"I appreciate you helping me out like this."

All those feelings Miriam had tried to command came flooding back—her old hopes and tender dreams. What was it about this man that made her knees turn to wet noodles with one piercing glance? Being Amos's wife would have been lovely, if they'd been more compatible, and if she'd been able to give him the family he wanted.

"*Yah*, it's not a problem," she said, and her voice sounded breathy in her own ears. Then she smelled the scent of bread, and she tapped him aside to pull on her oven mitts. Amos stepped back, his strong arm brushing against hers as he did so, and she swallowed hard, pretending that it didn't feel as sweet as it had.

She'd do her duty by her husband—in the kitchen at least—for these few weeks. And when she left, she'd be certain that he was fine without her. Maybe there was wisdom in *Mammi*'s request, after all.

Patricia Johns is a *Publishers Weekly* bestselling author who writes from Alberta, Canada. She has her Hon. BA in English literature and currently writes for Harlequin's Love Inspired and Heartwarming lines. She also writes Amish romance for Kensington Books. You can find her at patriciajohnsromance.com.

Books by Patricia Johns

Love Inspired

Redemption's Amish Legacies

The Nanny's Amish Family
A Precious Christmas Gift
Wife on His Doorstep

Montana Twins

Her Cowboy's Twin Blessings
Her Twins' Cowboy Dad
A Rancher to Remember

Harlequin Heartwarming

The Second Chance Club

Their Mountain Reunion
Mountain Mistletoe Christmas
Rocky Mountain Baby

Visit the Author Profile page at Harlequin.com for more titles.

Wife on His Doorstep

Patricia Johns

LOVE INSPIRED
INSPIRATIONAL ROMANCE

LOVE INSPIRED®
INSPIRATIONAL ROMANCE

Recycling programs
for this product may
not exist in your area.

ISBN-13: 978-1-335-48889-3

Wife on His Doorstep

This edition published by arrangement with Harlequin Books S.A.

For questions and comments about the quality of this book, please contact us
at CustomerService@Harlequin.com.

Love Inspired
22 Adelaide St. West, 40th Floor
Toronto, Ontario M5H 4E3, Canada
www.Harlequin.com

Printed in U.S.A.

"Who can find a virtuous woman?... The heart
of her husband doth safely trust in her."
—*Proverbs* 31:10–11

To my husband, who I love more than anything.

Chapter One

"*Mammi*, let me get that for you." Amos pulled his grandmother's mug of tea closer to her before she could rise to her feet to reach it. Outside, the day was chilly, the May sunlight drawing out the buds on the trees, but not warm enough for the sick old woman's comfort. She had a shawl around her shoulders, and Amos had put another one over her lap, but her fingers were still cold. He wanted to help…more than help, he wanted to make her well.

The sound of an engine drew their attention, and Amos rose to his feet and headed for the window. It was a taxi, and he couldn't see the occupant, but it was a blue dress that first appeared out the door, then a small traveling bag, and when the woman straightened and turned, bag in hand, his heart stuttered to a stop.

"Who's there?" *Mammi* asked.

He knew the woman very well, and at the sight of her, his breath turned shallow and his heart hammered hard to catch up.

"Amos?" *Mammi* said.

"It's my wife," he breathed.

Miriam Lapp tugged a black woolen coat closer around herself in the spring chill, and she stopped short when she saw Amos in the window. Miriam had changed a little since she'd left him ten years ago. Her strawberry blond hair was pulled back under her *kapp*, but one tendril fell free and it ruffled in the wind. She'd be thirty-five now, and she could still make his breath catch.

"Miriam is here?" *Mammi* asked, and this time she did stand up and her lap blanket fell into a pile at her feet.

"*Yah*, it looks that way," Amos said, and he headed for the door and pulled it open. "*Mammi*, you should sit down," he said over his shoulder, but his grandmother didn't listen.

Miriam headed toward him and came up the steps, then stopped. It was like the last decade just crumbled around him and he was left looking at the wife he'd vowed to love and protect all the days of his life...

"Hello," Amos said quietly.

"Hello, Amos." She didn't smile.

"It's been a long time," he said, his voice tight. He cleared his throat. "A very long time."

"*Yah*, I know," she replied. "You look..." She looked him over in a frank appraisal. "You look good, Amos."

"I've held together," he replied. "So do you."

She looked more than good—she looked beautiful in that way she always had. She'd never been an obvious beauty. Men didn't twist in their buggies to get a second look at her, and Amos had liked that. He'd never wanted a wife that other men gawked at. Miriam had a solidity about her, and a frank honesty that he'd been drawn to from the start. It was why he'd asked her to marry him after only knowing her for four days. They both wanted marriage and *kinner*, and he'd thought she'd make a fine wife. What was the point in wasting time?

"Can I come in?" Miriam asked.

"Yah." Amos stepped back, and he watched her as she came inside the house, unwrapping the shawl from around her shoulders. She'd put on a little weight in the last few years, and it looked good on her. But why was she here?

"Hello, *Mammi*," Miriam said, and she went forward to take *Mammi*'s outstretched hand. "I'm sorry to burst in on you like this."

"I'm glad to see you," *Mammi* said softly. "It's been…a while."

"Yah." Miriam released *Mammi*'s hand and glanced back at Amos. "I don't need to take up much of your time, Amos. I know I'm probably not welcome here—"

"Nonsense," *Mammi* interrupted. "You're Amos's wife, dear. You *belong* here."

Amos could hear his own breathing, and his head felt light. He'd had enough shocks for one day, and he eyed Miriam uncomfortably. Technically, *Mammi* was right, but the goodwill of extended family hadn't been enough to keep them together.

"Why have you come?" he asked at last.

"My *daet* passed away." Her lips quivered with repressed emotion. "Last week. A stroke."

"I'm sorry," he said. "I didn't hear." He looked futilely toward the folded newspaper, *The Budget*, that lay on the kitchen table. He hadn't opened it yet, but that was the best way he'd learn of anything happening in Miriam's hometown of Epson, Pennsylvania, where her father had lived and owned his businesses.

Miriam nodded and blinked back some tears. "*Gott* knew best." For a moment, there was some awkward silence. "Anyway, *Daet* left everything to my brother, Japheth."

"Everything?" Amos asked. "He didn't hold something back for you?"

She shook her head. "I thought he would have—"

So did Amos, for that matter. Her father, Leroy Schwartz, was a wealthy Amish businessman, and he had never made any attempt to help Amos and Miriam reconcile—at least no attempt that allowed Amos to have any self-respect. Leroy thought Amos wasn't a good enough provider for his daughter, and if he'd kept his married daughter home with him, enjoying a life that Amos couldn't hope to provide, then the least the old man could have done was leave her something in the will so that she could continue in comfort.

"Are you coming back, then?" Amos asked, uncertain how the question sounded, but it had to be asked. Her father was dead, and Leroy had been the one providing for her. As her husband, Amos was the one responsible for providing for her now, if she needed help.

"No, I'm not coming back to be a burden on you," Miriam said, and color bloomed in her face. "But when you and I got married, *Daet* gave us that commercial property in Epson as a wedding gift, and—" Miriam stopped. "And since *Daet* was running the place, anyway, all these years—it was only in our names on paper—"

"You want it back," Amos said.

"Yah..." She shrugged weakly. "I know it's crass, Amos, but it's the way I'll support myself, if you'll let me. Otherwise, I'd become your problem."

Miriam smiled slightly, and Amos's gaze moved toward that small travel bag. She hadn't come prepared for a long stay, so it seemed as if she were partway joking. Amos hadn't heard anything about that strip of stores since she left. Her father had put them into both of their names, but he'd continued to manage them—not that Leroy Schwartz would have trusted him with it. That was more of an insurance for his daughter in the old man's eyes.

"Yah..." Amos shrugged. "It's yours, Miriam. Do with it as you like. Your *daet* wanted you to have it, anyway, and I've never had anything to do with that property."

Besides, Amos had his own thriving carpentry business, and he wasn't a vindictive man. He and Miriam had both suffered enough.

"Do you know where the papers are?" Miriam asked hopefully. "I need to show them to Japheth and prove that strip mall belongs to me. He's already changing things, and he was about to evict some tenants, and—" She stopped. "I need to prove it's mine."

"They might be in the safe-deposit box at the bank," he said. "I don't remember if that was where I put them or if they're still around here somewhere—but the bank is already closed for the day."

Miriam's face flushed again, but she didn't ask him if she could stay. She dropped her gaze, then nodded twice.

"I'll come back tomorrow, and maybe we could go to the bank together, then," she said. "I'll get a room in town, and in the meantime, if you'd be willing to look through your papers here—"

"Come back?" *Mammi* interrupted. "Why would you go to some hotel in town when your home is right here?"

"*Mammi*'s right," Amos said. "You can stay here until this is sorted out. It's your home, after all."

Even if she'd never appreciated it. Even if she'd been so anxious to get away from it that she'd left important documents behind in her rush.

"Thank you," Miriam said, and she glanced around uncomfortably. "I'll try not to be in your way, Amos. I'll do the cooking and cleaning while I'm here, of course, and—"

"Amos, would you go see to the chores outside?" *Mammi* said, her voice silencing Miriam.

Amos met his grandmother's gaze, irritated. Was she really trying to get rid of him?

"If you don't mind, dear," *Mammi* said, softening her tone. She cast him an apologetic look.

"*Yah*, of course," Amos replied.

"I need a word with you alone, Miriam," *Mammi* said, and her voice firmed. "This requires some privacy between women."

Miriam and Amos both looked back at *Mammi* now, and Amos couldn't help but wonder what *Mammi* had to say that he couldn't hear.

Amos pulled his coat on and headed outside without another word, but as he shut the door behind him, he couldn't help but cast another curious look over his shoulder. *Mammi* had never been the take-charge sort around his house, and the last several years, he, Noah and Thomas had been taking care of her in her old age. She didn't have the same strength or even eyesight anymore.

What could *Mammi* have to say to Amos's estranged wife at this late stage? Miriam was his wife in *Gott*'s eyes, and in the community's, but she hadn't been a wife to him in a very long time. Whatever *Mammi* had to say to her could be said in front of him, couldn't it? Unless *Mammi* didn't want to embarrass Miriam any more than she had to when she lectured her about her moral, wifely duties. Who knew what passed between women when men were out of earshot?

Amos sighed and headed in the direction of the stables. He might as well muck out some stalls.

Besides, having Miriam here for a day might help with *Mammi*. She'd need some care that only a woman could provide, and both Noah's wife and Thomas's had small *kinner* of their own to care for. If Miriam could pitch in, it would help.

Gott, *heal my grandmother*, Amos prayed in his heart as he pulled open the stable door. This was the same prayer he'd been raising up since that doctor's appointment yesterday morning. They were all in *Gott*'s hands, but right now Amos needed *Mammi*'s sensible advice and gentle ways more than ever.

Because Miriam had just arrived, and that had sent his heart for a different kind of tumble.

Miriam looked toward the closed door, then toward the old woman. *Mammi*, or Mary Lapp as the rest of the community knew her, looked smaller somehow, and more fragile. But at her age, frailty could creep up faster than any expected. It had been a long time since Miriam had been in this house or even looked into this old woman's face…and she fully expected a lecture.

Miriam was not a good wife.

"Sit down, dear," *Mammi* said.

Miriam pulled up a chair opposite *Mammi* and sat, perching on the edge. Miriam pressed her lips together, bracing for the onslaught.

"I'm sorry for your father," *Mammi* said quietly.

"Thank you." Miriam felt the tears rise again. Her father's death had been a shock to everyone. "We didn't see it coming."

"No, we don't tend to," *Mammi* said. "You know, at my age, you look at me and see a withered old woman. But I don't feel old. My joints feel old, and my hips sure do, but my heart doesn't. I look in the mirror, and it's like I see a stranger with wrinkles and white hair. In here—" she placed a hand over her chest "—I'm as young as you."

Miriam nodded. "They say time flies."

"It does," *Mammi* replied. "It feels like yesterday your Amos was a little boy at my apron. Now he's your husband."

Mammi looked at her meaningfully. Here it was— the lecture.

"*Mammi*, I know this didn't turn out the way anyone hoped," Miriam said. "But it's complicated. I'm not some horrible woman who uses and abuses her own husband."

"Then help me to understand," *Mammi* said. "Why can't you and Amos be together? It isn't like either of you can remarry and try this again. He's the only husband you have."

"We don't get along, *Mammi*," Miriam said quietly. "He wants *kinner*, as all Amish men do, and I'm afraid to have them. The thing is, I was just as eager for a family as any other woman when we got engaged, but you know that my mother died delivering me. It was when my sister died with her second baby two weeks before the wedding that I got really scared... I didn't want to die giving birth like she and my mother did. Is it so wicked of me to think that I might have value aside from giving birth?"

Mammi shook her head. "Of course you have value in and of yourself. *Gott* created you in His image. And I had a good deal of trouble having babies, myself. You know about that. So I do understand."

"But Amos thought I'd get over it—he thought I was just grieving a sudden death in the family. He wanted me to have more faith—but it wasn't his life that was in the balance, was it?" Miriam's voice trembled. It was an old argument, but it felt fresh. "And I'm too bold and forthright for him. It was a good thing when I came looking for a husband in Redemption, but not once we were married. I was supposed to change who I was."

"That first year is difficult," *Mammi* said.

"More than difficult," Miriam replied. "He couldn't get along with my father, and I couldn't be the woman he wanted. I'm good with numbers, with business, and I learned a lot from my father—none of which Amos wanted from me. He wanted *kinner*. He thought I was someone different when he married me, and I take responsibility for that. All the same, we made a mistake.

We jumped into marriage because we were both lonely, and we thought it would be enough. It wasn't."

"And yet, you're still his wife," *Mammi* said seriously. "And there are certain duties—"

"I'm not sacrificing myself to have a baby!" Miriam burst out.

"I'm not asking you to," *Mammi* said. "But there is something I need you to do, and it's important."

What would it be now? Some ploy to bring them back together and show them that a lifetime of tolerating each other under the same roof was better than what they had now? Miriam wasn't a good wife. She couldn't settle into the Amish rhythms of marriage, babies and motherhood. But she did have other plans.

"*Mammi*, please, this is between me and Amos, and—"

"I'm dying."

The words hit Miriam in the chest. She blinked. "What?"

"I'm dying," *Mammi* repeated. "We found out yesterday. I've been going for tests and I have some very aggressive cancer."

"You could still beat it," Miriam said with a shake of her head.

"It's very advanced." *Mammi* pressed her lips together. "No, I think it's best to accept the inevitable. This is bad, Miriam. And I only have a couple of weeks left."

Somehow, Amos's grandmother had seemed like she'd outlive the rest of them. She was always so strong—emotionally and physically. But then, Miriam's father had been a strong, barrel-chested man, too, and he'd died. Human beings were all more fragile than they might like.

Miriam shook her head. "I don't know what to say. I'm so sorry… I—"

"*Gott* doesn't make mistakes," *Mammi* said gently. "Isn't that what you said earlier? *Gott* counts out days. He lays them out before us, and when our time to go home to Him comes, we go."

Miriam met the old woman's watery gaze, and for a moment, they were both silent.

"Are you scared?" Miriam asked weakly.

"A little," *Mammi* replied. "I've never died before." The old woman smiled at her own gallows humor. "I don't know what that will feel like. But I do know that I'm in *Gott*'s hands, and I feel confident in that. I'm looking forward to Heaven. I'll see my own dear husband again, and the babies who died in their infancy— I'll finally hold them again. I didn't have an easy life, my dear. All of my children died before me, so I'll be grateful to see them again."

"I hope I have your courage when the time comes," Miriam said.

"This brings me to my request," *Mammi* said. "Right now, I have some strength to dress myself and wash myself, but the days are coming very quickly where I will need a woman's help. I know I could ask any number of relatives in Ohio or Florida once I tell them the news, but they're far away, and it wouldn't be easy on them. Besides, I'm asking you."

Miriam felt her heart skip a beat, and she licked her dry lips. This was a heavy request—one she couldn't deny if she were part of the community here, but she wasn't any longer. "Why me, *Mammi*? I'm not exactly part of the family anymore."

"Technically, you are," *Mammi* replied. "But more than that, my grandson needs your support, too. I've been the woman caring for his home these last ten years, and I've helped him in raising two teenagers to manhood. I've been the one to encourage him and remind him that *Gott* loves him still, even when life is hard. And I'm about to die. He needs support through this, and I want you to help him."

He'd raised teens—she'd heard the rumors about that. Her husband had taken in two boys.

"Would *he* want that?" Miriam breathed. "Because I don't think he looked overjoyed to see me, *Mammi*. It's been a long time. I'm sure there are other people who are closer to him."

Mammi was silent, her blue eyes meeting Miriam's until Miriam dropped her gaze uncomfortably.

"You left him, Miriam," *Mammi* said firmly. "*Yah*, marriage was hard. It was hard for both of you, but you left this home, and you doomed that man to a lonely life without a wife by his side. He didn't leave you. There is a distinction there."

Guilt welled up inside of Miriam's breast, and she swallowed. "I tried, *Mammi*."

"I know, dear." *Mammi*'s voice softened. "And I'm not asking you to come back and live as his wife. All I'm asking for is that you stay for two weeks—maybe three—and you help Amos through my death. That's all. As his lawful wife, I think you could do that much for him." *Mammi* deflated back into her chair. "But you can decline. I'll understand, and I'll never mention it to Amos."

Miriam sucked in a breath. The old woman watched her fixedly, and Miriam knew that what *Mammi* asked was reasonable. This was how the Amish community survived—they pitched in and helped to care for each other. They didn't have old-age homes, they had family, and Mary Lapp didn't have any living children to step in. Marriage was a lifelong commitment, and there was no divorce permitted. *Mammi* was only asking her to do her Amish duty in a time of need.

"I'll need my own room," Miriam said. "I know we're married, but Amos and I can't share a room."

Mammi smiled at that. "Of course, dear. I'm not asking you to keep up appearances, just to support Amos. That's all."

There were footsteps outside, and the side door opened. Amos came back in, and he glanced at them, then went to the mudroom sink to wash his hands.

"Am I all right to come back in?" Amos asked.

"You're the man of his house," *Mammi* replied softly. "You come and go as you wish."

Miriam smiled weakly at that. *Mammi* had always been a strong spirit whose words were sometimes a little closer to the Amish ideal than her actions. She'd most certainly booted Amos out of the house for the conversation.

"*Mammi* has asked me to stay," Miriam said.

Amos eyed her for a moment, then his gaze slid toward his grandmother. "What?"

"For two or three weeks," *Mammi* said. "I need help

that only a woman can provide, Amos. And I've chosen Miriam."

Amos nodded, but worry creased his brow.

"*Mammi*, if this is some attempt to reunite Miriam and me—"

"Nonsense," *Mammi* said with a small shrug. "Do you really think I'd use the last few weeks of my life to meddle in yours?"

"It had occurred to me," he said with a faint smile. "But we're adults who know what we're doing," Amos added. "We've tried this, *Mammi*. More than once."

"Sometimes things change," *Mammi* said quietly. "That's all you can really count on in life, isn't it?"

Amos looked over at Miriam and they exchanged an uncertain look. Even knowing what *Mammi* was very likely trying to do, how could Miriam turn down a dying old lady who'd always been nothing but kind and good to her? And as much as she hated to admit it, Amos was going to need help getting through this— *Mammi* wasn't wrong there.

"I'll stay in the guest room, if it's available still," Miriam said. "And we're understood that there is no pressure here. I'm just here to do my duty by you both and help for a little while. Then I'll take my paperwork and go back home. You don't have to worry about that."

Amos cleared his throat. "So *Mammi* told you what the doctor said?"

Miriam nodded.

"Okay, then," Amos said with a sigh. "I guess it's decided."

Miriam looked toward the kitchen. There were dishes to wash, and dinner would come soon enough.

She grabbed a blue apron from a peg on the wall and tied it around herself.

"I'll cook and clean while I'm here," Miriam said. "So you won't have to worry about that. I'll even get some food put aside into the freezer. You still have one in the basement, don't you?"

"Yah," Amos said.

Other people would come by with food, as well. Amos would be fed after his grandmother passed.

"I'm ready for a nap, if you two don't mind," *Mammi* said.

"Let me help you to bed," Amos said, and as *Mammi* pushed herself to her feet, he went to her side, steadying her.

Miriam was back in her married home, and it was strange how little had changed around here. Granted, she could see the corner of a bed in the sitting room, making things easier for *Mammi*, but the rest of this house remained the same.

She touched a blue, chipped teapot on the counter, and her mind swept back to the day she'd moved into this old house as Amos's wife. She'd been full of hope back then, and that blue teapot had been new—a wedding gift. She'd unpacked it, washed it and made their first pot of tea as a married couple. Amos had brought whoopee pies—the chocolate kind with the white, whipped centers. She loved them, and he knew it. Their first meal together in that house had been whoopee pies and hot tea.

Ten years ago, she'd still thought that *Gott* had blessed her with a home of her own, and that her talents would be celebrated by this quiet, new husband of hers...

Miriam picked up the warm teapot and emptied it into the sink. The teabag fell to the bottom of the sink with a splat.

Ten years ago, Miriam had still thought that those wedding vows guaranteed some sort of special blessing onto the well-meaning couple—a hedge of protection, or a deeper well of wisdom...but she couldn't have been more wrong.

Miriam had made a mistake to marry Amos, and as a good Amish woman, there was no way to undo it. But she could help now—for a couple of weeks while they needed it most.

Chapter Two

"*Mammi*, what are you doing here, asking Miriam to stay?" Amos asked as he helped his grandmother lower herself onto the side of her bed.

The stairs had gotten increasingly difficult for her in the last couple of months, so Noah and Thomas had helped him to bring her bed downstairs. There was no extra bedroom down here, so the sitting room had turned into her private room for the time being, and it saddened him to think that when the sitting room was returned to its proper purpose again, *Mammi* would be gone.

"I'm doing what I should have done a long time ago," *Mammi* said. "I'm trying to help you two reach some peace."

"So you admit to meddling?" he asked with a tired smile.

"It isn't meddling exactly," she replied. "It's making you face each other. I have no power over what conclusions you'll come to, but you need to face her, Amos."

Amos sighed. His grandmother might be right.

"Now?" he asked sadly.

"If not now, when?" she asked. "I wouldn't have written to drag her back here, but she showed up on the doorstep, and that felt…providential. Sometimes *Gott* is working in mysterious ways, and you have to let Him."

There was no arguing with *Mammi*. She was convinced that *Gott* was always working, always moving, and every little coincidence was orchestrated from above. And after his parents passed away—first his father, and when he was a teenager, his mother—*Mammi* had been the one to take him into her home and raise him. So he knew his *mammi* very well, and to try to convince her that, just this once, *Gott* wasn't up to something…it wouldn't work.

"Do you need anything, *Mammi*?" he asked. "A glass of water?"

"No, no," she said, lying down on her pillow. "I took my pills earlier. I'm fine. I just need rest."

Amos looked back at *Mammi* for a moment, and she looked so small, so thin. She used to be a plump grandmother who plied all the kids who came over to play with Amos with pie and sweet, Amish peanut butter sandwiches. When he'd been struggling with his father's gruff, overly strict ways, it had been *Mammi*'s softness that had been a respite for him. She'd made him believe that there was still beauty in the world, despite the difficulties in his home. She used to be a source of quiet wisdom, which included some memorized scripture or a line from a hymn.

But the years had caught up to *Mammi*, and for all she'd done for him in years past, she needed him now to take care of her. But she was trying to do something good before she left them all—he just wasn't convinced that she was doing the right thing. She could focus on someone else, or even use these last weeks for herself...

Would she die disappointed? That thought gave his heart a squeeze.

When he emerged into the kitchen, Miriam looked up from the sink full of dishes she was doing.

"I know this is awkward," she said, then turned back to washing out a pot.

"Yah," he agreed. "But I don't think I could turn *Mammi* down right now."

"Me, neither." Miriam didn't turn toward him again. She continued scrubbing, her shoulders hunched up as she worked.

Amos stood there for a moment, wondering if he should go find some work outdoors, but he couldn't quite bring himself to leave just yet. There was something about seeing his wife's familiar figure at the sink that had him rooted to the spot.

How many times had he dreamed of this—one more chance to fix their relationship? But it was different in the light of day.

"Miriam," he said.

"Hmm?"

"What are you going to do?" he asked. "After you leave, I mean."

"I told you," she replied. "I've got a strip mall in Edson that brings in an income." She glanced back. "If I can find the documents that prove it's mine."

"Ours," he qualified.

Some color touched her cheeks. "Yes, ours."

Amos sighed. "Dry your hands. Come on."

He headed for the staircase and didn't even wait to see if she followed him, but he heard her footsteps as she caught up, and they hit the top stair side by side. Amos opened his bedroom door and headed straight to his closet. He pulled down a cardboard box. When he turned back he saw Miriam standing tentatively in the doorway.

"You're my wife," he said. "I imagine you could step foot in here without fear of scandal."

Miriam smiled faintly at that, then stepped inside. "It feels strange. That's all."

It felt a little weird to him, too. This used to be their bedroom together, and even when they were fighting and going to sleep back-to-back, as far from each other as possible, it had still been theirs. He put the box on the bed and sat down next to it.

"Are the documents in there?" she asked.

"I don't know," he replied. "But I haven't gone through it since you left, so…"

He still remembered that horrible day when he'd come back from the shop and found the house cleaned to a shine, and a letter on the kitchen table. His stomach clenched at the memory. It had been four days before he'd been able to cry over his loss, and that had happened in the stable, sitting on a hay bale and sobbing his heart out into his own calloused hands.

Miriam's gaze dropped to the box, and she sank onto the bed on the opposite side of it. Amos opened the flaps. Inside, there was an envelope and he opened it and slid out their marriage certificate.

"There's that," he said, passing it over.

Miriam took it wordlessly. He rummaged through

and found an old tax return, and a few pens with their names and the date of their wedding printed on the side. For what that was worth now.

There was an old *kapp*, a little dusty, and a few hairpins. He passed them over, then pulled out a comb that had been hers, too.

"You kept all this?" she asked at last.

"It didn't feel right to throw it out," he said, and his gaze dropped to the *kapp* in her hands. "It was still perfectly good, that *kapp*. And the hairpins. I mean… they were still—" he was just repeating himself now, but she'd always left him a little tongue tied "—they were still good."

As if that explained why he'd kept it all. Whatever their marriage had become, when Amos had married Miriam, he'd been full of hope, and those last feminine touches around his home had reminded him of the life he'd dreamed of but never got to enjoy with her.

The last item in the box was a half-finished wooden box. He'd started the engraving on the edges and never finished it. Miriam picked it up and turned it over in her hands.

"It was going to be for our anniversary," he said.

Miriam nodded. "Where did we go wrong, Amos?"

"We're just very different people," he replied with a shrug. "And I drive you crazy."

She smiled faintly at his humor, and they fell silent for a moment. She'd driven him crazy, too, for the record. She hadn't understood how he thought or what hurt him any better than he'd understood her. It was like everything she did was geared to prove him less of a man somehow. But had she meant to do it, or were they just horribly matched?

"The papers I need aren't here," she said.

"I haven't thrown anything out," he said. "They're around somewhere. We'll keep looking. And we can check the safe-deposit box at the bank tomorrow."

Miriam nodded. "Thank you."

"When you find them…and when you go back," he said, "will you be happy?"

"I think so," she replied. "I want to build up my business. My *daet* started with one store—did you know that?"

"*Yah*, you told me," he replied. Repeatedly. Her *daet*'s story was like a legend for her.

"Well, he built it up—store by store—until he owned most of the street. And I want to do that—start with the strip mall that I have, and manage it well so that I can buy another business to actually manage. The secret is in having more than one business—more than three actually. Leasing out the strip mall is my first, but if I can make a decent profit, I'd like to buy something more traditional."

"Like?" he asked warily.

"I don't know—something truer to our Amish roots. I was thinking of opening a fabric shop, or a bakery. Maybe a carpentry shop. I could buy another piece of property on another street. I don't have to be there to physically run the new business, but I could manage it—I can hire people for the day to day operations. But I'd need to choose the type of business carefully so that I could make enough to give decent wages. That's important to me—that people are able to make enough."

"I pay my guys well," he said.

"That's a good thing." She nodded. "If you were ever looking to sell—"

Amos pushed himself to his feet. "Sell? You think I'd give up Redemption Carpentry?"

The business that *he'd* grown from the bottom up? Was he supposed to give up, or something?

"No, just—" She shrugged. "I was just saying. I didn't mean anything by it."

"If I was ever looking to sell, you'd be the last person I'd sell to," he added.

"Why?" she demanded, rising to her feet to match him. "Because I'm a woman?"

"Because you spent every single day of our marriage comparing me to your father," he snapped. "Your *daet*, the business genius. Your *daet*, the respected entrepreneur. Your *daet*, who was a humble, Amish man despite the fact that he owned a good chunk of that town."

That last part was meant to be ironic, because her father hadn't been humble in the least, but people had been forced to make him feel like he was. He owned too much—they depended on him. Charities went to Leroy Schwartz first, because his support would be the most crucial. Miriam had been used to a certain amount of deference that came from being Leroy's daughter, except Amos hadn't deferred to her. He'd been her husband, and he'd expected her to trust him.

"My carpentry shop never did measure up to your father," he said.

"That's not true," she replied. "You were only starting out. Of course you wouldn't have what he did."

"It certainly wasn't enough for you," he said. "You

didn't marry me for the man I was. You married me for the man you thought you could make me into."

"I married you…" She sucked in a breath and her eyes snapped fire. "I married you because I was an idiot who thought marriage was the answer to everything. I was wrong about that."

They both were. He'd thought that a decent Amish woman in his home would bring happiness, too. He'd thought that if he could find a woman of faith like his *mammi*, that he could sidestep the misery his parents had endured. He and Miriam had both been naive.

"My father was a good man," Miriam added. "And he left big shoes to fill."

"Your brother will be fine," Amos said with a sigh. "He's inheriting enough that he can afford to make a few mistakes and not suffer from it."

"I was talking about myself." She met his gaze with a glittering glare. "I'm stepping into his shoes."

"You're going to try to be like him?" Amos asked in disbelief. "That's a man's role. What about your home?"

"Here?" she asked uncertainly.

"Anywhere. Your kitchen. Your quilts—"

"I'll do both," she said, then she shook her head. "Maybe I won't quilt, Amos. I live in my father's house with my brother and his wife, and we've managed to keep house so far."

"And that's enough for you?" he asked. "A shared house with your brother, and a sprawling network of businesses that call you 'ma'am' like some Englisher woman?"

"Englisher?" She seemed to hear the insult in that word. "You call me that? I'm a Schwartz. My family has been Amish since we came over from Switzerland. Being successful doesn't make me any less Amish!"

And he wasn't as successful, just a small-business owner who made enough to pay his workers and a little extra to set aside for retirement. That was the hint, but he wasn't going to do this. They'd fought enough to last a lifetime.

"I'm not trying to argue," he said, moderating his tone. "I'm sorry."

Miriam crossed her arms over her chest, not seeming to have heard his apology. "I won't have *kinner*, Amos, but I'll still grow something that will outlive me. I'll still contribute to my community with jobs and quality goods, and I'll make a space for myself. Sometimes that space takes a little money in order to carve it out. That's just life. But I won't be ashamed of success, my own or my father's."

Amos ran a hand through his hair. "We're Amish! It isn't supposed to be about money!"

"Money is a tool, Amos," she said. "It isn't supposed to be about the *love* of money. There's a difference."

Was there, though? He didn't exactly think that poverty was a virtue, but Jesus had talked about the wealthy and eyes of needles, hadn't He?

"I don't want to fight with you," she said.

"*Yah*, me, neither," he said, but his words sounded angry, even in his own ears. What was it with this woman that could rile him up this way? He was normally a calm and reasonable man, but staring Miriam down like this, he felt like all of his rational ways deserted him.

Miriam had a deeper, more challenging kind of attractiveness. Her eyes had a depth to them that he'd never seen in another woman. And the way she angled her chin when she was holding back an opinion had always stuck with him...

Funny how their disparate personalities had led to as many kisses as arguments—as unhealthy as it seemed to be, their attraction was linked to the fighting. That wasn't Amish, at all. He caught her gaze, and her flushed cheeks brought out a glitter in her eyes. There had been a time when he'd been able to kiss those pink lips...but not now. Fighting and making up couldn't support a relationship for any length of time. Amos's parents seemed to find a balance of arguments and then gentleness, but he couldn't have called his mother happy exactly. And it wasn't like he wanted the relationship his parents had had—he was trying to avoid it.

"If we keep up like this, we'll only upset *Mammi*," Miriam said.

She had a point, and Amos let out a long breath. "*Yah.* Let's stop fighting about all the old problems and get along for a couple of weeks."

"Okay. I agree," she said.

He held out his hand, and she took his. Her hand was slim and soft, and he shook it gently. "And don't worry—we'll find your documents."

"I hope so."

"They're here, Miriam." He glanced around. "Somewhere."

Couldn't she trust his word with just one thing?

"Now, I have to go see Noah and Thomas," he added. "They know about *Mammi*, but we need to discuss some things together, and they'll want to come see her. Can I let you take care of things here while I do that?"

"Of course," she replied. "I'll make a big enough dinner that if people come they'll be fed."

"Thanks…"

And just like that, he had a wife in his home again. For all Miriam drove him crazy, he was grateful to have someone here to help him, even if she did stir up a stew of powerful emotions. But that had to stay safely beneath the surface until she'd left again. He didn't have the strength to face both his grandmother's passing and his unrealistic hopes at the same time.

His heart had never been safe with Miriam.

Miriam peeked under a clean dish towel at the rising little domes on the baking pan. She was making a batch of buns to go with a large pot of beef stew. It would stretch to feed extra people, and it generally tasted good. But Miriam had never been a fantastic cook like her friends had been. She'd been the one who could do math in her head faster than her brothers could on paper, and her father had proudly used her as his "Amish calculator." She'd had other skills, even back then.

And it was hardly fair that her *daet*, who had encouraged her in this, who had been so proud of her business acumen, hadn't left her anything more than the property bestowed on her at her wedding. She was thirty-five years old, and if her *daet* had wanted her to become more feminine and focus on the cooking and cleaning, he shouldn't have focused on teaching her the family business skills. She wasn't a pet to teach to do tricks—she was a woman who'd believed that she had her father's respect. That will that left everything to Japheth had been *Daet*'s judgment from beyond the grave—he'd cut her down to size, just not to her face.

Miriam took the lid off the bubbling pot and fished a piece of beef out to test its tenderness with a fork. It wasn't soft enough, and she dropped it back in.

"Did I sleep long?"

Miriam looked up to find *Mammi* in the doorway, her *kapp* a little askew.

"A few hours," Miriam replied. "Here—I'll help you with your *kapp*."

She crossed the room and adjusted *Mammi*'s *kapp*, pulling out the hairpin and replacing it gently.

"Thank you, dear," *Mammi* said. "Where did Amos go?"

"To see Thomas and Noah," she replied.

"Ah. Yes." *Mammi* didn't say more than that.

"I heard some rumors about my husband taking in some boys," she said.

"*Yah*. They're the sons that Amos never had."

Miriam felt a stab at those words—the sons she'd been unwilling to provide apparently.

"They're grown now," *Mammi* added. "He took them in after you left, when they were teens in need of a proper Amish home. They were so scared. So alone."

"Where were their parents?" she asked.

"Their father died, and their mother went English. She wanted them to go with her, but those boys were devout and they wanted to stay. So she agreed so long as they stayed with Amos. She trusted him. So Amos stepped in, and he raised them the rest of the way. Their mother visited, and she eventually came back to the community. But we all became a family by choice."

"That's…quite lovely," Miriam admitted.

"Yah," Mammi said. "We love those boys—well, men now—very dearly. And they're both married and growing their families."

As Amish people did. Or as Amish people were supposed to do. There were always a few who didn't follow the mandate to be fruitful and multiply. Miriam rubbed her hands down her apron.

"Mammi, I'm going to bring a more comfortable chair into the kitchen for you," Miriam said, and she headed into the sitting room to gather up one of the upholstered chairs that had been shoved against a wall to make room for the bed. She dragged it out to the kitchen, then fetched an ottoman to go with it.

Mammi sank into the chair and allowed Miriam to pull the ottoman closer. Then the old woman looked wistfully toward the kitchen. "You look like you're cooking for a crowd."

"People are going to want to see you, *Mammi,*" Miriam said. "They love you. I'm just preparing…in case people come by."

Mammi nodded. "Funny how quickly the time passes. I still feel like I could be thirty-five, you know. Well, maybe not thirty-five. That's how old you are, isn't it? And you seem almost like a baby to me." She laughed softly. "I feel like I could be fifty, though. Eighty-eight creeps up when you don't notice."

"You're eighty-eight?" Miriam asked. She'd never known *Mammi*'s age before.

"Yah." Mammi turned toward the window, and her

gaze grew sad. "You don't want to get to my age and have regrets, Miriam. You want to take hold of these years and live them to the full. There's no going back. Once they're gone, they're gone."

"Do you have regrets?" Miriam asked.

"A few," *Mammi* said, and she looked toward Miriam. "I wish I'd enjoyed my husband a little bit more. I didn't realize I'd lose him so young. And I wish I'd argued with my sister less. I wish I'd known how to help my son, who was addicted to drink and gambling… I just didn't know. Nothing I tried worked."

Miriam was silent. Perhaps no one was completely free of regrets. She had a few of her own, the biggest one being her wedding. Miriam went back to the counter, checked the rising buns and decided they were ready for the oven. She added a few more coals to the fire, and then slid the pan of buns inside.

"There is a customer who won't pay Amos," *Mammi* said.

"What's that?" Miriam closed the oven and straightened.

"At the shop," *Mammi* said. "There is a customer who won't pay him. They promised to pay up, and never did. Amos keeps thinking that because it's a big company ordering furniture for a show home that they can be trusted."

"Why are you telling me this?" Miriam asked with a shake of her head.

"Because I thought you might have some insight for him," *Mammi* replied. "While you're here, you might help him out a little bit."

Miriam chuckled softly. "*Mammi*, if only you knew

how much Amos would hate to have me meddling in his business."

"Oh, I know just how much he'd hate it," *Mammi* replied, and a smile flickered at the corners of her lips. "It would still be good for him."

The women exchanged a smile and Miriam rolled her eyes. "You're not sounding like a good Amish woman, *Mammi*."

"Ah, but I'm a very good grandmother," she countered.

Outside, Miriam heard the crunch of buggy wheels and the clop of hooves. She went to the window and looked out. That wasn't Amos, or at least the first buggy wasn't Amos. It was a younger man with a blond-haired woman at his side. There was a little girl peeking over their shoulders, and the woman seemed to be talking to the child very seriously.

People were coming, but so was some help in the kitchen. Another buggy pulled into the drive behind the first one with another couple, the man's marriage beard still short, and the woman had a baby in arms. Was Amos really leaving her alone to host people she didn't know? Her heart sped up, but then she saw the third buggy—and it was Amos.

He sat tall, and his dark gaze was locked ahead of him. He always had been a good-looking man—those broad shoulders, the strong hands. He held himself with more confidence now, and she found it hard to tear her gaze away from him.

But she did, and she commanded her heart to stop that hopeful pattering. She might be able to feed people, but that was where this ended. This was Amos's life, and Amos's chosen family.

A few minutes later, the women came inside with the little girl and the baby. They gave Miriam a brief hello, and then went to *Mammi*'s side, bending down to speak with her quietly. Miriam watched them—there were some tears, some reassurances, and *Mammi* kissed the baby, and the little girl tried to crawl onto *Mammi*'s lap, but her mother stopped her.

Then the door opened again and the men came in, the buggies now unhitched, it would seem. They were all somber and quiet, and when Amos looked across the kitchen, he caught her eye and held it.

"I would also like to introduce you to my wife," he said, raising his voice so that it reverberated through the room.

The kitchen silenced, and all eyes turned to her. At first, no one moved, then the woman with the little girl rose to her feet and crossed the kitchen.

"It's nice to meet you at long last," she said. "We've heard about you."

Nothing good, no doubt. Miriam gave her a silent nod.

"I'm Patience," she added. "Thomas's wife."

Then one by one, the others came by to do the same—Thomas and Noah, and then Noah's wife, Eve, with their baby boy, Samuel. The little girl was named Rue, and she stared at Miriam with wide, wary eyes.

"Come, Rue," Patience said, holding out her hand. "Come say hello."

Rue came to Patience's side and whispered loud enough for Miriam to hear, "She's the bad lady…"

Patience's face flooded red. "I'm sorry, she sometimes says things—"

"It's all right," Miriam said. "I'm sure people have talked. I understand."

This was what she'd agreed to, wasn't it? She'd said she'd stay for a few weeks, and that would entail running into people who would have heard about her. Women who left their husbands were considered dangerous, on pretty much every level.

"Let us help you with the food," Eve said, and she passed the baby over to her husband.

"Rue, you can help set the table," Patience said, casting the little girl a smile.

Miriam looked at the other two women uncertainly. Would they hate her? Make sure she felt just how wicked she was in their eyes?

Amos came by the stove, his large frame filling up the kitchen. The women moved to the side, slipping away to give them momentary privacy. Amos lifted the lid of the pot to look inside the bubbling, savory depths, and Miriam watched him uncertainly.

"It looks really good, Miriam," he said, his voice low enough for her ears alone. He replaced the lid. "I appreciate you helping me out like this," he added. "Truly."

And all those feelings she'd tried to command came flooding back—her old hopes and tender dreams. What was it about this man that made her knees turn to wet noodles with one piercing glance? Being Amos's wife would have been lovely, if they'd been more compatible, and if she'd been able to give him the family he wanted. But he'd found a way around it, and he'd had that family without her.

She should be glad for him.

"*Yah*, it's not a problem," she said, and her voice sounded breathy in her own ears. Then she smelled the scent of bread, and she tapped him aside and pulled on her oven mitts. Amos stepped back, his strong arm brushing against hers as he did so, and she swallowed hard, pretending that it didn't feel as sweet as it had.

She'd do her duty by her husband—in the kitchen at least—for these few weeks. And when she left, she'd be certain that he was fine without her. Maybe there was wisdom in *Mammi*'s request, after all.

Chapter Three

Amos led the family in worship that evening around the kitchen table. It was comforting to be all together, sharing the sadness and the prayers as a family. They all took turns praying for *Mammi*, even little Rue. They prayed for healing, and for comfort, and for reassurance for her that whatever happened, *Gott*'s will would be done and that *Mammi* would be protected from pain. *Mammi* asked them to sing her favorite hymn, too, and when they were done, *Mammi* was tired again and the women, Miriam included, helped her to get into her nightclothes for bed.

The men were left alone in the kitchen, Noah holding his infant son in his arms. Samuel was asleep, nestled against Noah's chest. Anyone just seeing this young father for the first time would never guess that this baby wasn't biologically his. He'd met his wife when she was eight months pregnant, but for Noah, there was no difference, and *Gott* had knit them together into a family more truly than DNA ever could. It was similar to the way *Gott* had made Amos, Noah, Thomas and *Mammi* into a family, too, and Amos had been so deeply thankful for what *Gott* had given him these last few years.

The men rose from the table and moved toward the windows. The sun had set, and the first few stars were piercing through the dusk.

"I don't know what I expected from Miriam, but she seems nice," Thomas said.

Amos looked over at the younger man. Thomas had a reddish beard and a more confident way about him now that he was a married man.

"That was never the problem," Amos replied. "She's a decent person."

"What *was* the problem, then?" Noah came up next to them, gently patting his son's diapered rump.

Amos sighed. "We're very different, and we just couldn't seem to get along. She didn't want *kinner*, either, and—"

"She didn't?" Thomas's eyebrows went up. "Really? Even now?"

"*Yah.* She's got a family history of trouble in childbirth, and it scares her," Amos said. "But it wasn't that, even. I mean, we could have adopted. She's from a wealthy family, and I don't think she realizes just how privileged she was. She was always trying to improve me, and I...hated it." He felt some heat hit his face. "I'm not explaining this well. We didn't get along. That's all that matters, and without *kinner* in a home, there isn't much reason for us to stay together and drive each other crazy, is there?"

"Do you think you might try again to make it work with her?" Thomas pressed.

"No." Amos shook his head. These men were both

young, and they'd married women who were well-matched to them.

"She came back, though," Noah said. "She could have left again if she didn't care."

"I think she does care," Amos admitted. "She wouldn't have agreed to stay and help *Mammi* if she didn't, but it doesn't change the complications between us. I tried to fix things a year after she left. I wrote her some letters, and I went to speak with her father."

"And?" Noah asked.

"And…it didn't go well. Her father thought I was beneath Miriam and he said that he'd encourage her to go back to me if I could prove I was a better provider than I'd been," Amos said.

"A better provider." Thomas's lips turned down.

"I had the carpentry shop, and I was building it up," Amos said. "That wasn't enough for a Schwartz, it seems."

"Did Miriam know what he said?" Noah asked.

"I told her. She defended her father. Even when that man was fully in the wrong, she would defend him and insist that I respect him. I couldn't keep fighting and pushing for something that would never work. I told her if she wanted to come home, she knew where I was. She never came."

"Until now," Noah said softly.

"She came for some papers," Amos said with a shake of his head. "Not for me. It was *Mammi* who asked her to stay. We know where we stand, Miriam and me, and we don't need to keep breaking our hearts afresh every decade."

The men fell silent. Amos didn't have any reassurances to give to Thomas and Noah.

"You two married the right women," Amos said. "I made mistakes, and so did Miriam. But you two can learn from us, and love your wives well. Don't let bitterness take root in your marriages—do whatever you can to keep things sweet between you."

"It's good advice," Thomas said quietly, and they all seemed to sink into their own thoughts.

Patience was the first one to come back into the kitchen with Rue at her side. Patience slid a hand into the crook of Thomas's arm and the couple exchanged a sad look.

"We'd best get home," Thomas said, and he shook hands with Amos and then Noah. "Rue here needs her bed."

As if on cue, Rue's mouth cracked open in a big yawn and she rubbed her eyes.

"*Yah*, of course," Amos replied.

"I'll go get our buggy hitched, too," Noah said. "Are you okay tonight, Amos?"

"*Yah*, I'm fine," Amos said. "The doctor gave *Mammi* pills to help her sleep, and Miriam is here, so…"

Noah and Thomas both looked toward Amos at mention of his wife, but this time there was just sad acknowledgment. The best of intentions weren't always enough.

When the buggies were hitched, Amos watched as they made their way out into the evening dusk, their headlamps bouncing as they went over some bumps and headed up to the main road. Noah and Thomas would be fine—they had wives to comfort them, and *kinner* to remind them of the next generation. This difficult time would be a little gentler for them because of the women at their sides.

"Are you okay?" Miriam asked, and it jolted him out of his reverie.

"Yah." He nodded.

"Mammi's sleeping now," Miriam said. "She seems comfortable."

Amos looked down at Miriam and let his gaze move over her face. He wanted to remember her like this— when she'd stayed for a little while to help them.

"Thank you for this," he said. "I'm not sure how I'd be dealing with this without you."

"Someone else would be here—a family member from Ohio, one of those women who were here tonight, perhaps."

"Still, it was you who was here, and I'm grateful," he said.

Miriam smiled at that. "You're welcome."

She passed him and headed to the counter. She began piling up dishes, and Amos joined her. They started the water in the sink, and Amos got a dish towel to dry while she washed.

"People are going to talk now that I'm here," Miriam said.

"Yah," he agreed. "They already are."

"Oh?" She glanced up at him, and he noticed the wariness in her eyes.

"Mostly they want to know why we aren't together," he said. "They like you."

She rinsed a bowl and handed it to him. "What did you tell them?"

"That we've gone through all of this before, and we don't need to do it again every decade," he replied.

"I like that." She cast him a tired smile. "That's a good answer."

"Do you still not want *kinner*, Miriam?" he asked. "Even at this age, when we don't have much time left to make it happen?"

Miriam sighed. "I've seen specialists. I was having some medical issues, and they were connected. I asked about the likelihood of me suffering from the same problem my mother and sister did—it was curiosity mostly. They said they recommended that I not get pregnant. That wasn't a problem. I wasn't with my husband, anyway, was I?"

She rinsed another bowl, then a plate, and piled them on the dish rack next to him.

"So you were right in being scared when we got married," he said.

"Yah."

Amos was silent. He'd spent a great deal of time and energy trying to convince her that she didn't need to worry and that they should start their family. He'd been so sure that he'd been right, too. Apparently, that had been foolish on his part.

"I'm sorry about that," he said. "I don't think I took it seriously."

Miriam shook her head. "It's fine."

But was it? If he'd reacted differently, would they have found a way to stay together? He'd been so sure that she was just overreacting to a family tragedy. He'd known he should have taken her more seriously in general—at least, that was the conclusion he'd come to over the years. When a woman said she wasn't happy, a man should take that as seriously as a fire alarm.

"If I hadn't pressured you to start a family—" he started.

"Don't do that to yourself, Amos," Miriam said. "This wasn't about *kinner*. We could have found a way to adopt—you certainly did."

"Then what was it about?" he asked.

"We're very different, you and me. And I didn't realize how different when we got married. I mean, would you have really wanted me involved in Redemption Carpentry?"

"I built up that business from nothing," Amos said. "I started it in my shed in the evenings while I worked a day job at a factory. I worked until I could barely stand some nights, getting a job done so that I could keep my reputation. I didn't need help, or advice. I didn't need you reporting back to your *daet* to have him judge me from Edson."

Miriam nodded, but didn't answer.

"Are you saying you wanted to help out at the business?" Amos asked. "That would have made you happy?"

Miriam turned and fixed her gaze on him. "I'd have liked to be the manager."

Of *his* shop. She gave him a rueful smile.

"Right now, I have a strip mall to lease out and plans for a business to start up," Miriam went on. "I won't have to ask permission to run it as I will, and *that* makes me happy. I'm my father's daughter, Amos. I have business in my blood, and I want to see what I can do when I'm not being held back by well-meaning men."

"Like me," he said.

She shrugged. "Maybe. And like my brother."

"You think you'll do better than your brother?" he asked.

"I know it." She didn't sound like she was bragging, either, just factual.

"Your father seemed to want you to take on a more feminine role," he countered. "Why else would he not give you any more in the will?"

"I agree," she said, and rinsed another dish, then pulled a fresh pile of dirty dishes into the sink. "He did seem to want that. But I don't."

Amos sighed and took another dish to dry.

"So stop beating yourself up about all those years ago," she said, and she smiled over at him. "Even if you'd been a little more sensitive back then, I'd still have driven you crazy."

"Is that supposed to comfort me?" He chuckled.

"Yes," she said, and she smiled. "Oh, Amos. We're ten years older, ten years wiser, and life hasn't gotten any simpler, has it?"

"It doesn't seem like it," he agreed.

"If I had met you under different circumstances, I think you and I might have been friends," she said.

"You think?" he asked doubtfully.

"Actual friends," she said. "No threat of marriage on any horizon. I think we might have debated things and disagreed and stomped off…and still respected the other's opinion. Maybe if we had neighboring shops or something."

"Would you have married a different kind of man?" he asked.

A richer man was what he meant. A more successful man.

"Me?" She laughed softly. "I wouldn't have been marriageable anymore, Amos. I refuse to have *kinner*, and I'm too stubborn in everything else. No, I would have stayed single." She glanced up at him. "You would have married, though."

Miriam was right. He would have. He'd have found a sweet woman who wanted babies and family and faith... and he would have loved her dearly for all of his life, and been grateful for the home he went back to every day. And the deeply ironic thing is that even if he'd married a different woman who would have made him happier, he would have thought back about the serious daughter of that Amish businessman and remembered the depth in those dark eyes... Even if he'd never married Miriam, she would have been in his head.

Miriam rinsed the last dish and handed it to him, then pulled the plug and dried her hands.

"Let me show you to your room," Amos said.

What they might have done no longer mattered. They'd locked themselves into this marriage, and no amount of what-ifs made any difference at all.

The next morning, Miriam stood at the kitchen counter with individual containers of hot stew in front of her. Amos had left early for work since he'd wanted to finish up a project, and he'd eaten a small breakfast with the promise that Miriam would bring them a hot lunch later in the courting buggy Amos kept for *Mam-*

mi's use. She and Amos would also take the opportunity to go to the bank's safe-deposit box and check for those documents. She'd feel better when they were in her possession once more.

She was already feeling rather domestic in her duties here at the house, but her mind kept skipping ahead to the carpentry shop. She was curious about it—the kind of business Amos had built for himself.

"How well does the shop do?" Miriam asked *Mammi*, who was seated in her comfortable chair pulled up next to the window.

"I wouldn't know exactly," *Mammi* replied. "Amos doesn't tell me those things."

"Right…" He wouldn't. That was the men's world, and they took care of those burdens alone. "But the business has a good reputation around town?"

"The best," *Mammi* replied. "Those men are very skilled. Amos made all the furniture in this home."

Miriam smiled. "*Yah*. I remember. Just before we married."

"That's right," *Mammi* said. "Amos's shop is known for their beautiful work. You should be proud of that." *Mammi* cast her a meaningful look.

"It isn't my work to be proud of," Miriam replied. She knew what *Mammi* was getting at—trying to give her a personal connection here. It wasn't so simple to patch things up, though.

"Where do they advertise their business?" Miriam asked. "On the local radio? In magazines?"

"They don't. They hardly need to," *Mammi* said. "Besides, most Amish people around here don't trust ads.

They trust friends and family. That's how you spread the word—let it go naturally."

That didn't apply to the Englishers, though—how could they hear about the shop if there were no ads? Englishers would travel for an Amish-run shop that delivered quality goods. But it wasn't her business—literally or figuratively.

Miriam dropped her gaze. "As long as the business is doing well. That's all that matters."

"Well…" *Mammi* paused, seeming to measure her words. "I do worry sometimes…"

"About what?" Miriam asked.

"I mentioned those customers that are giving Amos trouble about paying," *Mammi* said. "Most people are honest and willing to pay the agreed price, but some aren't." *Mammi* lifted her gaze. "Some push and pressure and complain so much that a decent man like Amos, who is dealing with a sick grandmother, might just give in."

Mammi stared at Miriam hopefully, and Miriam met her gaze, frowning. *Mammi* had apparently picked up more than she wanted to readily admit. The men's responsibilities might not be the women's business, but everyone was affected by them.

"What's going on?" Miriam said.

Mammi sighed. "I shouldn't meddle. I know that."

"But it's bothering you, all the same," Miriam said gently.

"The order they're working so hard to complete today—that is the one that hasn't been paid in full, and the customer was late in getting them the down payment," *Mammi* said. "Amos has been particularly worried about it. I overheard him talking to the boys—sorry, Noah and Thomas—and they all agreed it was a problem. It's a big enough order that if they don't get paid, they can't pay back some of their own creditors."

"How big is the order?" Miriam asked.

The number that *Mammi* said made Miriam suck in her breath.

"And you think they won't pay?" Miriam asked.

"Amos thinks so," *Mammi* replied. "Me? I just listen to them talk. But with my illness, I'm not sure Amos is at his best. If they don't get paid for this one, it'll be hard for Amos. Very hard. I know this isn't what matters at a time like this—money certainly isn't a faithful person's priority—but Amos has worked too hard to have his business driven under by unprincipled people. I'll be with *Gott*, but he has to face the coming months. He's a man with ideals, and he lives by them...but I worry."

"What would I do about it?" Miriam asked.

"I don't know," *Mammi* said, and she shrugged weakly. "Maybe nothing. But could you perhaps pray on it while you're driving out to deliver their lunch?"

Miriam took the courting buggy down the still-familiar roads that led to the town of Redemption. The afternoon was warm, and Miriam couldn't help but enjoy the grass-scented breeze. Bees buzzed around the wildflowers that grew up in the ditches at either side of the road, and beyond the barbed-wire fences, cows grazed and looked up at her passing buggy with large, liquid eyes.

Mammi had asked her to pray...

Lord, I feel like I haven't prayed enough to ask for

Your guidance. I came out here to find the documents, and I didn't even bother asking what You thought of it. And now I feel like I'm getting entangled in Amos's life all over again, and I can't tell if I'll only make things worse.

Because when she left the first time, she'd ripped both of their hearts to shreds, and she'd promised herself she'd never do that again. Whatever they'd hoped marriage would be, they'd both been wrong. But in her own defense, she'd gotten a lot of advice from older married women telling her that if she just followed expectations, all would be well. A good man—any good man—would be a good husband, she'd been told.

Just don't nag him.

That little piece of advice had come from a very happily married aunt, and it had turned out to be the most difficult to follow. Was it nagging to tell him her opinion about things? Was it nagging to point out what she'd learned from growing up with an entrepreneur father? Was it nagging to mention when he could save some money, or take advantage of a deal? Even if it wasn't, that never seemed to do well for their relationship. Amos had been sensitive about his shop and about her father's opinions about him, and if she had to be honest, *Daet* had been rather terse and curt. But he was like that with everyone—and they'd respected his words because he was a man who knew what he was talking about.

Except for Amos. Amos had taken everything so personally, and he seemed to expect things from *Daet* that others didn't. And from her, too...

"I'm sorry I wasn't a better wife, Lord," she prayed

aloud. "But maybe I can help him now…in his time of sorrow. Maybe You can use me to ease his burdens a little bit, and maybe make up for not enough praying before I married him."

Because if she'd prayed hard back then and listened intently, God would have found a way to show her that this marriage wasn't His will. She was sure of it.

The town of Redemption had grown since she'd last lived here, and there were more Englisher tourists than she remembered, too. A group of women stopped on the sidewalk and took a picture of her passing buggy. She smiled and nodded at them, and they beamed back at her. If Edson could draw in more of the tourists, she could make use of this amount of passing foot traffic on a sidewalk…

But this wasn't about her, it was about Amos. Her own business plans could wait until she got back with her documents. Maybe *Gott* had brought her to Redemption for a reason… Maybe he needed her for a little while more than he realized.

Miriam parked her buggy behind the carpentry shop with her horses under a tarp erected for shade. A few yards away, there was a large box truck, the windows open and the driver eating a fast-food burger from the driver's seat. She eyed him as she got down from the buggy, then put her attention into her own business. There was a trough of water, and after the horses had drunk their fill, she gave them their feedbags. Then she looked toward the back entrance of the shop. Did she dare go in that way?

She sucked in a wavering breath.

No, she'd go in the front.

Miriam gathered up the wooden crate that contained the towel-insulated containers of stew, and she made her way between the buildings toward the front of Redemption Carpentry. An Englisher man passing on the sidewalk noticed her attempting to open the door, and he pulled it open for her. She smiled her thanks and headed inside.

Amos was at the counter, and two young Englisher men stood there with angry stances. They wore blue jeans and dirty T-shirts. One had a trucker's cap pushed back on his head.

"Our boss is waiting," the first Englisher was saying. "And we have a truck rented and waiting out back. This is costing us money. Who's going to compensate us for that?"

"I need payment," Amos replied.

"Our boss will send the check," the second Englisher replied. "But he wants to see the furniture himself and make sure the order is right before he pays you. It's only fair."

Amos sighed and rubbed a hand over his beard. "He could have come himself and seen to that."

"He's obviously busy with other things," the first man snapped. "Now, if you aren't going to release our goods, we're going to be letting other businesses know exactly how we feel about your shoddy service. That could tank a business of your size."

Miriam's heart pounded hard and she met Amos's gaze over their shoulders. She went to the counter and deposited the crate of food, then angled her head to the side.

"Excuse me," Amos said, and followed her a couple of yards away. "Everything okay?" he asked her.

"At home, fine," she replied. "But you can't release that furniture to them."

"Miriam, this isn't your business," he said.

"I'm just saying—they'll never pay. Their boss, or whoever is cutting that check, is not going to pay up."

"They'll pay," he replied. "It's just the way Englishers are sometimes—"

"Amos, listen to me," she said, reaching out and catching his arm. "I've seen this before with my *daet.* He always said that an item loses value in the customer's eyes once it's in their hands. The invisible boss won't pay the full amount—I can guarantee that."

"What makes you so sure, knowing absolutely nothing about this customer?" he demanded.

"*Mammi* filled me in," she replied.

"Forgive me, Miriam, but we don't worry *Mammi* with these things," he said with a sigh.

"Well, she worries all the same," Miriam shot back. "And according to her, you've been worried, too. I've seen this before. An item is worth the quoted price to a customer as long as that item has not been attained. The minute they have it in their possession, the value decreases for them—it's an emotional thing. They no longer feel the pressure, or the yearning for it, and they don't see why they should have to pay top dollar anymore. They'll offer you something less, and since they've already got the furniture, you'll have no choice but to accept it."

Amos shook his head. "He's paid the down payment."

"Can you afford to lose the rest?" she asked.

"I know what I'm doing," Amos said, and while his tone was even, she could see the annoyance flashing in his eyes. He pulled his arm free and headed back over to where the men stood, their backs to them. They appeared to be making a call on their cell phone now.

"…won't hand it over," the first man was saying into his phone. "What am I supposed to do, then?"

"So *Mammi* asked you to help with this?" Amos asked, looking back at her.

"Yah." She shrugged. "It's a tough time for you, Amos. It isn't shameful to accept help. Maybe I'm the last person you want it from—and I do understand that—but I'm here. And I'm offering. For whatever that's worth to you."

Amos's expression turned stony, and he paused for a moment, considering. Then he turned to the Englishers.

"I need the payment before I release the furniture," Amos said, raising his voice. "I have to insist."

Miriam couldn't help the smile that tugged at her lips.

"My boss is going to be furious," the first Englisher said, warning in his tone.

"It's just business, my friend," Amos said simply. "I can't let that furniture go without payment. When you can sort out the payment, then we can load up."

"We'll be back," the man growled, and they headed out of the store, the cell phone still at his ear.

Miriam eyed Amos cautiously. "That was the right thing to do."

"If it wasn't, I just lost a major sale," he said.

"If he's an honest businessman, he won't be offended

at you expecting payment," she countered. "I'm sure he expects payment for his services, too."

Amos ran a hand through his hair, then sighed. "I didn't know *Mammi* was worried. And I'm a little offended that she thinks I need help."

"She wants me to be a supportive wife," Miriam replied. "And in my opinion, that includes the business."

Amos regarded her thoughtfully for a moment. "You don't trust me."

"Your grandmother is dying," Miriam replied. "You're not at your best. That's understandable. *Mammi* wants me to help you, too, but I can't do that unless you'll let me."

Amos nodded slowly. "She could have asked anyone else…"

"We know what she wants," she said softly. "She wants to reconnect us, and while we both know it isn't that easy, if she knows that we're working together during this difficult time, she'll be comforted at the very least. She's worried, Amos, and if that relieves her worry…"

Their gazes met, and Amos sighed. He pressed his lips together, then dropped his gaze.

"All right," he said. "For *Mammi*. Will you help me out around here, Miriam?"

"Yah." She felt her eyes mist. "I'd be happy to."

"But you can only speak to me about your ideas privately. Never in front of my employees or the customers."

"Of course, Amos."

She'd get her husband through this difficult time, and maybe it could be penance for the rest of her mistakes.

While they hadn't been a good match romantically, Amos was still a good man, and he deserved support.

Maybe You brought me here at this time for a reason, Gott, she prayed. *Gott* sometimes worked in the strangest ways.

"Let's go to the bank," Amos said. "We'll check the safe-deposit box for those documents."

Those documents were her escape. When all of this was finished, she had a life and a business waiting for her in Edson. But when she left, she would feel better for having done her duty.

Chapter Four

Amos held the door for Miriam as they headed out of the shop and onto the sidewalk. It still felt like a dream that she was even here—close enough that he could smell the faint scent of vanilla in her hair from a morning spent in the kitchen as she passed through the door ahead of him.

He'd dreamed of her over the years while she was gone… Some dreams were just his frustration working itself out. He would dream of their arguments, of him stomping out the door to try and find some peace outside, and he'd wake up in a sweat, relieved that he wasn't actually pitted in some week-long mental struggle with his own wife.

Noah and Thomas used to tell him that he talked in his sleep—loud enough to be heard through the walls. He hadn't done that since he was a boy, and he'd been filled with all the anxiety of his mother's unhappiness. She'd been sad a lot—and sometimes as a child he'd watch her just standing there in the kitchen, motionless and so weighed down by unhappiness she looked like she might crumble.

"It's not your fault," she used to tell him. "It isn't your *daet*'s fault. I just have this cloud that seems to find me… That's all. It's just a cloud."

Back when his mother was consumed by her cloud and had crawled into her bed after her work was done to lie alone there, his cousin who slept over sometimes used to tell him that he talked in his sleep, too. There was something about the sadness he couldn't fix that had worked its way into his dreams back when he was a boy, and it seemed to come back again after Miriam had left.

But other dreams of Miriam had been softer and sweeter. One night, not too long ago, he'd dreamed of holding her hand, and feeling the softness of her skin, and smelling that feminine aroma of baking and sunlight that clung to her clothes and hair… He'd woken from that dream with such an ache of loneliness inside of him that he'd been forced to get up a full hour before sunrise, just to try and shake it.

And now Miriam was here, still smelling faintly of baking and sunlight. It was almost cruel that his dream of her had matched the reality so well. Couldn't *Gott* make this easier on him?

But maybe Amos didn't deserve easy. He'd married the wrong woman, and now he would pay. What a man planted, so did he reap. Did Amos have any right to ask *Gott* to change those rules on his behalf?

A man in a passing buggy leaned forward to openly stare at Amos and Miriam, and Amos sighed. That was

Isaiah Kemp, a local farmer who lived on his grandfather's land.

"We've been spotted," Amos murmured.

"I noticed that," she replied. "Sorry."

"It's okay. It was bound to happen sooner or later."

And people would ask questions. That kind of gossip would fly around town—Amos's runaway wife was back in town. They'd be wondering if Amos and Miriam were reconciling at long last, and then they could all discuss it afresh when she left again. As much as Amos hated being the topic of local gossip, he was glad he had a community that cared.

"What will you tell people?" she asked, glancing toward him warily.

"That we had some business together," he said. "It isn't really their business. What do you want me to tell them?"

"That we have some business together is fine," she said.

"Do you miss any of them?" he asked. "I mean— do you miss any part of living here in Redemption?"

Miriam's expression turned wistful. "I miss our first few weeks of marriage. That was a nice time."

Amos tried to remember those first few weeks. They hadn't known each other well, and there had been so many guests, so many invitations to honor after their wedding. Every Amish new couple was inundated with friendliness.

"We were so busy," he said.

"Too busy to fight yet," she said, and she shot him a smile. "I miss that—when people were happy for us, and the women were teasing me about learning to cook for you, and…and no one was mentioning babies quite yet."

"Yeah…" Come to think of it, maybe he missed those first few weeks, too, before either of them realized that this was a monumental mistake.

The bank was three blocks east of Main Street, and as they walked along side by side, away from the busy Main Street, Amos felt some of his tension fade. There were no buggies on this particular street, and the people who stopped to stare at them were tourists. He could handle the curiosity of strangers. Amos glanced over at his wife.

"So, do you have anyone discussing the fact you came to see me?" he asked. "Did you start any gossip in Edson by coming out here?"

She shrugged. "I might have. My brother knows I'm here, and he knows why. I called from the phone shanty yesterday so he wouldn't worry and left a message with an Englisher business. They'll pass it along—to more than my brother, I'm sure."

"He's really going to insist that you prove you own that strip mall?" Amos asked. It seemed petty, especially when Japheth had inherited everything else.

"Yah." She shrugged. "He thinks I should do my duty and come back to you."

Amos raised his eyebrows. "Really?"

Amos hadn't had a terribly warm relationship with his brother-in-law.

"Japheth said that *Daet* was wrong about giving you such a hard time, and that I should have come back and learned how to be a proper wife," Miriam said. "He said I should be minding a home, not a strip mall."

"Did he always think that way?" Amos asked. How long had Amos had support from her side of the family and not known it?

"Japheth never would cross *Daet* when he was alive," she replied. "But that isn't the first time my brother told me to come back to you. You should be grateful I don't let my brother bully me, or I might have been on your doorstep sooner."

Amos hadn't known that his brother-in-law had been encouraging her to go back to him—that was news. He tried to smile at her humor, but he wasn't sure he managed it. It wouldn't have been terrible to see her sooner…if she'd wanted to be a proper wife to him again.

"Maybe he meant well," Amos said quietly.

"I tried to be the wife you wanted, Amos," she said. "It didn't work. It's harder to change yourself than you anticipate. And my brother wants me involved in his business just as much as you want me in yours. That's all this is—I'm in the way."

Amos dropped his gaze. He couldn't argue with that. She had absolutely refused to stay in the home, and Amos took his role as man of the home seriously. It was his job to run the business and provide financially for his wife. Whatever it took to bring home enough money to keep them comfortable and pay his employees, he'd do it. She needed to trust him, just as he needed to trust the running of the home to her. He'd never tell her what to cook, or when to plant the garden, or when to harvest the vegetables. He'd never tell her how to arrange her own kitchen or when to air out the bedding. That was her realm.

Except they'd hardly known each other when they married, and she *hadn't* trusted him to take care of things.

Redemption Credit Union was on the corner, and Amos let his wife go inside ahead of him. There were no Amish people in the bank that afternoon, which was a relief. And they waited in the snaking lineup to get to a teller.

"Hi, Mr. Lapp," the teller said with a smile.

He didn't bother reminding her that she could just call him Amos. The Englishers had their own way, and she meant it as respect.

"I just want to get into my safe-deposit box," he said.

"Of course. Just a moment," the teller said with a smile. "I just have to sign out the keys."

"Do you…need to see inside the box yourself?" he asked Miriam, his voice low.

She cast him a small frown. "I trust you, Amos."

With this, perhaps. But she hadn't trusted him to provide for her.

"Mr. Lapp?" the teller said, coming back. "Just this way."

Amos went into the little sterile-feeling room beside the bank vault and he accepted his box from the woman with a nod of thanks. He put it on the table and opened it. He didn't keep too many things in the safe-deposit box—some business documents, some land deeds… And when he sorted through them, he didn't find the documents for Miriam's strip mall. He went through them again slowly, just to be sure, but they weren't there.

Where would those documents be? He hadn't seen them in years, and he never would have disposed of them.

When Amos relocked his box into the wall of the vault and came back out, he turned to the teller who had helped them.

"Thank you," he said. "Have a good day."

Miriam was silent, but she did look down at his empty hands and her disappointment was evident.

"They weren't there," he said as they came back out into the sunlight. "I'm sorry. It was worth checking, though."

"Do you have any proper filing system?" she asked.

"Of course," he replied.

"I mean for your personal documents," she said. "Because my *daet* always had a carefully organized personal filing system that was just as meticulous as his system for his businesses. He always said that—"

"Miriam." Amos's curt tone cut her off. "I know where *my* personal documents are. These are yours."

The distinction mattered, because he couldn't be blamed for misplacing her papers. She'd been the one who left so fast she'd left them behind, and he wasn't taking the blame for that.

"Fine." She pressed her lips together.

"Are you sure you don't have the documents with your own things?" he asked.

"I went through everything," she replied. "They aren't there. Trust me, it was the first thing I did. I didn't want to come here."

He felt the cut in those words. But this was hard for her, too, he realized. And now she'd given her word that she'd stay for a few weeks.

"We'll keep looking at home," he said.

She nodded. "At least we know they aren't in the safe-deposit box. That's something."

As they headed back toward Main Street, Amos looked over at her. The breeze was cool, and she rubbed her bare arms. His first instinct was to put an arm around her—it was what he would have done years ago if she were cold, but he mentally chastised himself for even thinking of it now. She might be his wife in name, but that was all.

"I'm sure we'll find the documents," he said. "It'll just take doing some searching together. We'll look when I get home tonight."

"Thank you, Amos," she said.

Amos was silent for a moment, and then he added, "I've done well with my business, I'll have you know."

He needed her to know this—that he wasn't some floundering fool, no matter how those unprincipled Englishers had made him look. He might not be the man to make her happy, but he was a man.

"Hmm?" Miriam's mind must have been elsewhere, because she looked over at him, mildly confused.

"I did well with my business," he said. "Since you left here, I've built up a three-carpenter operation. I'm well respected, and I pay my employees well. I believe in that, too—making sure Noah and Thomas can support their families on one job. I don't want them to have to look for work on their evenings in order to make ends meet."

"That's really good," she said with a gentle smile.

And he felt like a fool for even mentioning it.

* * *

Miriam's mind was on those documents as she made her way back to the buggy parking lot. If she couldn't find the document that signed that piece of property over to her, she *would* be Amos's problem. That hadn't been a joke earlier. Japheth had the official sales documents from when their father acquired the commercial property, and there were no copies of the papers that signed it over to her.

Was this her father's plan to send her back to Amos, after all? It didn't seem likely. *Daet* had been frustrated with her choice in husband. He might have liked Amos more if he'd been more deferential to *Daet*. But Amos was a man who stood tall—he was respectful, but he didn't take advice easily, and he didn't seem overly impressed with *Daet*'s accomplishments.

Not that *Daet* had wanted Amos to be in awe of him exactly. But Amos could have tried harder to win him over. Instead, Amos had simply gone about building his business the way he wanted to. With *Daet*'s advice, that carpentry shop could be three shops by now. But whenever Miriam had suggested that her father might have some ideas to help him, Amos would freeze up and refuse to hear her.

Miriam reached the buggy and stroked the gelding as she came up toward his head to remove the feed bag. She walked him to the water trough to let him drink before the ride home and waited as he did so.

"Miriam Lapp?"

Miriam turned to see a woman shading her eyes. She stood just behind the fabric shop, then she waved. It was Fannie Mast, one of Miriam's friends from that first year of marriage. She wished she could just duck out of sight, but she'd been spotted now. Miriam waved back.

Fannie headed in her direction, walking quickly with a smile on her face.

"Miriam!" she said as she arrived and enclosed her in a hug. "You're back! Praise *Gott*! We've all been praying for you and Amos to reconcile, and I have to say, my faith had gotten weak on the subject—"

"It's good to see you, Fannie," Miriam said.

"When did this happen?" Fannie asked, shaking her head.

"It...hasn't," Miriam said with a wince. "I'm here to find some paperwork, and I'm staying long enough to help Mary in her time of need."

"What time of need?" Fannie frowned. "Is she all right?"

"She's dying," Miriam said softly. "She doesn't have much time, and she asked me to help her until...until..."

Fannie's eyes misted with tears.

"Oh..." Fannie breathed. "I had no idea..."

For the next few minutes, they talked about *Mammi*'s illness and all the sadness that came along with it. Mary Lapp was a beloved member of the community, and everyone would want to help her, including Fannie.

"So you aren't home to reconcile?" Fannie said softly.

"No..."

Fannie nodded and swallowed.

"How are you doing, though?" Miriam asked.

"I'm good," Fannie said. "We have four children now—two boys and two girls." She smiled. "When you and I met, I was pregnant with Adam, and Silas was making our first cradle out in the workshop, re-member?"

"I never did meet your son," Miriam said.

Silas was Fannie's husband, and they'd been quite newly married when Miriam and Fannie had met and struck up a friendship.

"Time has certainly marched on," Miriam said. "That's wonderful. *Gott* has blessed you."

"I've worried all these years…" Fannie paused. "We used to…vent…to each other…"

Miriam knew what her friend was referring to, and she batted her hand through the air.

"Fannie, it's fine. We used to complain about our husbands to each other. Your secrets are safe," she said.

"We were wrong to do that," Fannie said. "I never breathed a word of it, except to Silas, of course—I tell him everything. But we should never have spoken of them that way. They're good men—honest, hardwork-ing, faithful. We never should have complained about their messy ways or the times they were thoughtless. I wasn't a perfect wife, either, you know! And after ten years of marriage, I have a better appreciation for the difficulties of that first year."

Miriam felt a wriggle of guilt.

"Fannie, we might have complained to each other," Miriam said. "But we also encouraged each other. You made me feel stronger—"

"Strong enough to leave him?" Fannie asked seri-ously.

"That wasn't your fault," Miriam replied. "Fannie, you fell in love. Silas adored you for years before he was old enough to court you, and you both fell in love with each other."

"So did you and Amos," Fannie countered.

"No," Miriam admitted. "We wanted to. We thought we would after we got married. We saw such wonderful potential in each other, but it just…it never happened. We drove each other crazy. We thought if we arranged things just right, we could have what you and Silas had—what other couples had. We wanted it, but we were wrong in getting married as quickly as we did. If we'd taken our time, we'd have seen the problems before we said the vows. So stop blaming yourself—this wasn't your fault. You made my life sweeter for being in it. I promise."

"You didn't last a year," Fannie said.

"Almost a year," Miriam said, as if that distinction even mattered.

"Can I tell you something?" Fannie said. "This is important, and I have been thinking about it the last ten years. I've been asking *Gott* to forgive me for my role in the breakdown of your relationship with your husband."

"Fannie…" Miriam said.

"The first year is the hardest," Fannie went on. "It just is. A wife will be upset because her husband isn't acting the way she expects him to act, and she might think that means he doesn't love her well enough, or that he's being selfish, or that he's choosing to ignore what she needs in the marriage. But that is seldom the case. Marriage is like any skill—like canning or quilting or gardening. It takes time to learn."

"*Yah*, I could see that," Miriam said uncomfortably.

She wasn't looking for marriage advice, but it looked like Fannie was intent on giving it.

"That first year or two of marriage is incredibly hard, and no one talks about that," Fannie went on. "The older couples just give you your space to figure things out between you. But I had to change, too. I had to learn how to bend for Silas. I was just as stubborn as he was!"

"What changed things for you?" Miriam asked.

Fannie was silent for a moment, then she sucked in a breath. "When you left."

"Oh…"

"*Yah.* When you left Amos, I felt just sick. The thought of leaving Silas made my stomach hurt to even think about, and it rattled me back to my senses."

So her life had been the morality tale to shock Fannie and Silas into each other's arms. Miriam wasn't sure she even wanted to know that.

"And then when Adam was born, we looked down at him, and we knew that we had to do better in our marriage…for our family," Fannie went on. "We sat down and we talked things out. I said what hurt my feelings, and he said what hurt his, and we both promised to do our best not to hurt each other ever again."

A baby—the one thing that Miriam wouldn't give Amos. It was bitterly ironic that a baby was their answer, but maybe that was appropriate. Silas and Fannie had been in love—the real kind of love where they got kind of mushy around each other. Amos and Miriam had been married—and love hadn't found them yet. It was all out of reach for them.

"I'm glad you sorted it out," Miriam said, and she felt a lump rise in her throat.

"That first year *is* hard," Fannie repeated. "If you'd waited longer—"

"I wasn't having *kinner*," Miriam said.

"I know you *said* that, but—"

"Doctors advised against it," Miriam said curtly.

"Oh…" Fannie nodded quickly. "I'm so sorry, Miriam."

But she was a mother of four children, and she'd never know what it was like to be a woman without them. Some sympathy didn't count for much. Back in their early days of friendship, they'd both been newly married and on equal footing. But children changed that dynamic between them. Fannie was a mother, and Miriam was not.

"It's all right," Miriam replied. "I've made my peace with it."

They were both silent for a couple of beats. Fannie kicked a little rock across the dusty ground.

"You said you and Amos weren't in love," Fannie said quietly.

She wasn't going to let this go… Miriam had agonized over it for long enough, and she'd answered so many questions in her own community over the years. She didn't want to discuss it any longer!

"We weren't," Miriam said firmly.

"We sometimes tell ourselves stories to make ourselves feel better," Fannie said.

"The fact that we didn't love each other doesn't comfort me, believe me," Miriam said with a sigh.

"You need to know this, Miriam. When you left, Amos was crushed," Fannie said earnestly. "Really crushed. He lost weight—we all worried about him, and Mary cooked all she could to fatten him back up again... But he was just...empty. Until he took those boys in, and then he had someone to care for again. They brought him back to life."

Miriam swallowed, silent.

"It broke his heart when you left him," Fannie went on. "So you claim you didn't love each other, but I daresay that Amos loved *you*." Fannie smoothed her hands down the front of her dress. "I'd better get back. I left the *kinner* with my *mamm* while I went for errands, and the littlest one, Priscilla, was just wailing when I left, so I need to get back."

"Of course," Miriam said.

"I'm glad I saw you," Fannie said. "And I'm going to be honest with you—I'll be praying that you and Amos reconcile. I won't be praying behind your back."

Miriam smiled faintly. "It was nice to see you, too."

When Fannie left, Miriam got up into the buggy and flicked the reins. She was eager to get away from here, back out onto open road where there was no more threat of meeting well-meaning old friends.

The balance between Miriam and Fannie had certainly changed. Back when they'd been confidantes, Miriam had been the stronger one of them. Miriam had been a few years older, she'd had a stronger personality, and she'd come from a family that had been very successful. Fannie had been younger, meeker, and she'd looked up to Miriam in a lot of ways. They'd both been new wives, and somehow, Miriam had been the "expert" on life.

Fannie didn't seem to look up to her anymore... She

was now the mother of four—with both marriage experience and advice. Miriam was the one who'd failed.

The horse moved onto the road, and she urged them toward the traffic light. It was green, and she leaned forward to look both ways as she came to the intersection, and then flicked the reins as they continued forward.

Forward—always forward. That was how she lived her life.

Fannie had said that Amos had been heartbroken. And while her own heart squeezed in response to that mental image of big, strong Amos losing weight and growing thin, it didn't have the effect that Fannie would hope.

Miriam wouldn't come back home to Amos, because she knew something that Fannie refused to accept— Miriam and Amos weren't good together. And if she came back the way Fannie was praying for, then she would only end up breaking Amos's heart all over again.

She *did* care about Amos's happiness. She did… enough to never attempt to reconcile. He deserved some peace.

Chapter Five

Amos headed back into Redemption Carpentry, a frown on his face. Miriam's opinion of him had always been a sensitive spot for him. Back when they'd gotten married, he'd wanted her to see the able provider he could be, but all she ever seemed to see were the places where he might be able to improve.

The ridiculous thing was, he was the most successful he'd ever been right now. His business was doing very well, he had Noah and Thomas working full-time with him and he was well-respected in the community. Amos had nothing to be ashamed of, yet faced with his own wife, he still felt like he had something to prove to her. And every time he tried to show her what he'd accomplished, it fell flat.

If he were smart, he'd just stop trying.

Amos headed through the empty showroom and into the back shop. Noah and Thomas were both bent over some sanding, and they looked up when he came in.

"Is our customer's truck still back there?" Amos asked.

"No, they left," Noah replied. "Are you sure about sending them off like that?"

"Not really," Amos replied, and he felt a wave of irritation. "Miriam said that her father had dealt with people just like them, and this was the way to handle it."

"And she'd know?" Thomas asked, squinting.

"She'd know how her father handled things, *yah*," Amos said as he put his hat onto a peg on the wall.

"That's a lot of money to be playing with," Thomas said. "If the buyer doesn't come back—"

"It's a lot of money to play with if he decides not to pay us the full amount, too," Amos replied. "She's right. If they decide not to take the order, then we'll sell the pieces individually. We'll get paid for it, just a little more slowly."

Still, he'd been anticipating that large check—he couldn't deny it.

"Wollie Zook put in an order for a kitchen storage cupboard," Noah said, turning back to his sanding.

Wollie Zook was a friend of Noah's back when they were *kinner*, and Wollie had gone English some years ago when he married an Englisher girl. They had four *kinner* of their own, and now they were living in the Amish area again.

"So Natasha is really converting to Amish?" Thomas asked.

"*Yah*, it would seem so," Noah said. "Last time I was there, she was in a *kapp* and apron. Her mother-in-law was teaching her how to sew dresses for the girls."

Amos let out a low whistle. No one had seen that coming—when a man went English for a woman, he didn't normally bring his whole family back with him.

"It's not easy for her," Noah went on. "Natasha is an English speaker, and the Dutch isn't coming very naturally to her. She's trying, though."

"How can she do the baptismal classes if she can't speak it?" Amos asked.

"Wollie went with her at first and was translating, but that was disruptive," Noah replied. "So the bishop is doing that particular baptismal class in English for her sake."

"That's nice of him," Amos said.

"If you want to bring someone into the fold, you have to make room for them," Noah said.

"Amen to that," Thomas murmured, and Amos glanced at the younger man. Thomas was sensitive about making a welcoming place for Englishers—his daughter was an Englisher girl and Dutch was her second language, too.

If they wanted to bring Wollie Zook back into the Amish community, then they had to make room for Wollie's wife. She was so very English…everything about her was different—the way she spoke, the way she stood, the way she looked at people so directly. The way she parented was just…louder. An Amish mother could murmur a remonstrance and have her child obey, but Natasha could be heard giving a lecture to her *kinner* all the way from the road.

"Patience is teaching her some basic Dutch," Thomas said. "But Rue keeps trying to compete with her, and I don't think it's fun being shown up by a five-year-old."

Amos chuckled. "Maybe she just needs friendship."

Noah and Thomas both nodded at that.

"This might sound crazy…" Noah looked up. "But I

think that Miriam and Natasha might actually get along. I think they both could use a friend."

"That's not a bad idea," Thomas agreed. "Sometimes the oddest combinations can make for lifelong friends."

Amos rubbed a hand over his beard. Was Miriam lonely? The thought tugged at his heart.

"She hasn't been back in Redemption for years, right?" Noah said. "Does she want to connect with any old friends?"

"She's been avoiding them," Amos admitted.

"Then she might appreciate a new friend," Thomas said.

"She's not staying," Amos reminded them. "She's here for a couple of weeks, and then she's going back."

Still, the thought of his wife's potential loneliness had softened a part of his heart. She'd always been a little bit on the outside of things. When they were married, they'd been arguing a lot, which meant that she didn't have that soft, comforting home with him. She had a few friends, but she didn't know anyone well—the friends she'd grown up with and her family were in Edson. Add to that, she was so different—something he only really noticed properly after they were married. She was stronger, more focused, more stubborn than the other women seemed to be. Miriam was more of everything.

"Are you sure you want her to leave?" Thomas asked.

Amos sighed. "It isn't about that."

"How is it not?" Thomas asked. "She's your wife. If you wanted her to stay—"

"It isn't that simple," Amos said. "Besides, she

wouldn't want to be at home. She'd want to run the shop."

The men exchanged a look. So they were finally understanding what he was getting at.

"Like, she'd run the front of the store?" Noah asked. "That might not be a bad idea. As it is, we have to run back and forth to serve customers and take orders while we're working. If we had someone who could stay out front and help customers, someone who couldn't be pushed around—"

"She'd want more than that," Amos said. "She'd want to change how I run things."

"What makes you so sure?" Thomas asked.

"I know *her*."

Amos wasn't in the mood to debate this. He knew his wife far better than Thomas and Noah were giving him credit for. He and Miriam had already fought battles that these young men had no knowledge of.

Maybe they were right about one thing, though. Maybe Miriam could use a friend while she was here—someone to distract her from his life a little bit.

The bell above the front door tinkled, and Amos headed for the showroom. When he got there, he saw the owner of the show homes standing with his arms crossed over his chest, looking around with a frown. He was a portly man with a cowboy hat and a large buckle, and when Amos came into the room, his gaze snapped up.

"Hello," Amos said.

"Mr. Lapp," the man said with a tight smile. "I'm not happy to have to come down here myself, I'll have you know. When I sent my men to pick up the order, I expected you to release it."

"I expected payment," Amos replied quietly. "I'm running a business here, Mr. Boone. I can't release the furniture without payment."

"You and I had an agreement," the other man said irritably. "I came to an Amish business because I thought my handshake would mean something here. I came for the old-fashioned moral fiber."

Amos didn't answer. He wasn't going to argue the morality of a handshake right now. A handshake only meant something when two men knew each other.

"Fine." Mr. Boone sighed, and he pulled a money order out of his pocket. "Here it is, in full. But I'll need to take a look at the furniture before I hand this over."

"Perfectly fair," Amos said. "Right through here. We have everything ready to load up. Do you have the truck here?"

"It's waiting around back."

Miriam had been right, it seemed. This Englisher businessman was ready to pay up, if Amos put his foot down with him. And looking at him now, Amos had a suspicion that once the man got the furniture, the payment wouldn't have been quite so prompt. Amos pulled out the paperwork for the order and nodded his head toward the back door.

"I have the order outlined right here," Amos said. "We can take another look at it together."

As Amos ushered the man through the back, he felt a wave of relief.

Thank You, Gott, he prayed. *We needed this.*

And maybe, just for today, he'd needed Miriam, too.

* * *

That evening, after they closed up shop, the men stood in the back room, their hats on their heads and the crate of rinsed, empty dishes from Miriam's hot stew all ready to go. It had been a productive day, and with that payment from the big order in the bank deposit envelope, Amos felt like they'd be all right. At least he'd be able to tell *Mammi* that she need not worry about it anymore.

"I'm tired," Noah said. "I'm looking forward to Eve's good cooking." He winced. "We could bring you some dinner, Amos."

"No, no," Amos replied. "My wife will have cooked."

The words came out more casually than he'd even intended. It had been so long since he'd been able to say anything like that, and he felt his face heat.

"Give *Mammi* our love," Thomas said.

"And ours, too," Noah added.

"Of course," Amos said. "I'd better get back. *Mammi* gets really tired in the evenings, and I want to be able to spend as much time with her as I can tonight."

"We're praying for her," Noah said. "And for you."

"Thank you." It meant more than the younger men might know, but in times like this, Amos wasn't expecting healing so much as he was longing for *Gott*'s comforting presence. "I'm going to go to Blueberry Bakery before I leave so I can bring *Mammi* some whoopee pies," he added.

"She'd like that," Thomas said.

"*Yah*, she would."

"We'll hitch your buggy so that you can leave right

away when you get back from the bakery," Thomas said. "It's the least we can do."

Amos felt a lump rise in his throat. These were good men, and he was glad to claim them in his makeshift family circle.

So Amos started up the road at a brisk pace, his heart heavy in his chest. He wanted to bring *Mammi* whoopee pies to make her smile, but these weren't only *Mammi*'s favorite treats, they were Miriam's, too. The first night they spent in their own house, Amos had made sure to have a box of whoopee pies from Blueberry Bakery, because Miriam loved them. He could still remember how she'd looked with a touch of cream at the corner of her lips and her eyes sparkling with happiness.

He pushed back the memory. *Mammi* loved whoopee pies, too. What Amish person didn't? If he brought those pastries home, would Miriam think he was trying to remind her of something?

He felt a tickle of nervousness at that thought. Maybe he was...

Regardless, Amos owed Miriam his sincere thanks today, and he ruefully acknowledged that *Mammi* might enjoy his humbled position with his wife even more than she'd enjoy the whoopee pies.

Dear, sweet *Mammi*.

She always was a matchmaker at heart. If only her last attempt at bringing a couple together could have some hope of working out, because *Mammi* would really enjoy that.

Amos would have to make do with whoopee pies.

Miriam stood at the kitchen counter peeling potatoes. It was a job she could do without even thinking, her fingers knowing the work so well that the pile of peels grew steadily without her hardly noticing.

On the porch, *Mammi* was sitting in the rocking chair chatting with a neighbor, Doris, who had stopped by to see her. The two older women's voices came filtering back through the house with the grass-scented breeze, soft and warm. They were talking about people the used to know years ago… "That Yoder boy, the one with the leg brace," and "the King family from Indiana—the ones who sang so beautifully." Miriam smiled wistfully. It was good that *Mammi* could have time with her friends remembering the richness of her life.

Outside the kitchen window, a neighbor boy was cutting the lawn with a push mower, the blades whisking through the grass. He ducked his head as he worked, his straw hat pushed back so that his glistening forehead was exposed. She watched him work for a couple of minutes, in the way she watched all children these days. If *Gott* had given her a different constitution, she might have had a strong, strapping boy like this of her very own.

But *Gott* didn't make mistakes, and she wasn't going to waste her time railing against Him. So she turned back to her cooking. Dinner tonight would be chicken, mashed potatoes, gravy and some canned green beans from last year's garden. Tonight she had a feeling they could all use a little comfort on their plates, and nothing seemed to feed heavy hearts better than chicken dinner.

The visit with Fannie had been on Miriam's mind all afternoon. Fannie and Silas had obviously worked out their difficulties, and there was a disparity now between Miriam and Fannie. Miriam had been strong back when she and Fannie had been friends—she'd been confident, sure of herself…and she'd been very sure that Amos was wrong. Fannie had been less certain of herself, more worried about what her new in-laws thought of her, and more heartbroken every time she and Silas had an argument.

And in Miriam's humble opinion, Silas had been in the wrong, too. He hadn't been taking his young wife's feelings into account. He'd been demanding and unwilling to bend. But they'd sorted things out apparently. They'd finally found a way to understand each other, after all.

Today, Fannie had been the stronger one, more sure of herself, and perhaps for good reason. The goal had been to have a happy marriage, not to go back to her father's home in disgrace, even if she did help grow a business. Comparing herself to her old friend, she felt embarrassed. How many diatribes had Miriam gone on that Fannie would remember now in a much different light? How many silly things had Miriam said about what made a marriage work that Fannie would shake her head about?

That was one problem with being opinionated and talkative—the Bible said that "In the multitude of words there wanteth not sin: but he that refraineth his lips *is* wise." In the multitude of words this time, there had been a whole lot of foolishness, and Miriam's face felt hot even now thinking about it.

Outside, she heard the clop of horses' hooves and the crunch of buggy wheels along the gravel drive. She looked out the window to see Amos's buggy pull up next to the stable. Amos said something to the boy with the

push mower, and the boy grinned up at him and nodded. Amos always had been good with children. They
liked him.

Miriam turned back to peeling potatoes into a big
black pot, the strips of potato peel dropping to a bucket
on the counter next to her. By the time Amos had finished with the horses and his footsteps sounded on the
steps outside, Miriam had finished with the potatoes
and set the pot on the stove to boil.

The side door opened, and Amos came inside, a bakery box balanced on one palm. Miriam put the lid onto
the pot and shot him a hesitant smile.

"It smells good," Amos said.

"Thank you," she replied.

He put the box onto the table, and then went back
into the mudroom. The water turned on as he washed
his hands, and she stood there, eyes on the box, waiting for him to come back out.

"So, how did it go at the shop?" Miriam called.

Amos came out of the mudroom, still drying his
hands. He tossed the towel into a hamper by the door.

"Fine," he replied.

"The business that owed you money—I imagine the
manager called you?" she said.

"No, he didn't call." Amos met her gaze with that
calm, reasonable way he had that had always driven her
crazy. He knew what she was asking.

"Oh… No?" Had she gauged that wrong?

"They did come back and pick up the order," he said.

"Did they pay?" she demanded.

Amos smiled. "*Yah*. They paid."

Was that so hard to tell her? She shot him an irritated look. "Good. That's what I wanted to know. The full amount?"

"What if it weren't the full amount?" Amos asked, crossing his arms over his chest. "What would that mean to you?"

"It would mean you were taken advantage of," she replied. "And I'd ask for his phone number to speak to him directly. That would be unethical business, and if he wanted to play fast and loose with businesses in this area, he can find himself with a very bad reputation in these parts. As it is—"

"He paid the full amount." Amos picked an apple from the fruit bowl on the table and took a crunching bite.

Was this a game for him?

"Why wouldn't you just tell me that?" she said.

"Why does it matter so much to you?" he asked. "I've kept myself in business for the last twenty years without your help or input. I'm sure I can continue on my own."

"It's the principle," she said. "I don't like seeing rich men taking advantage of a small business. It's not right. Of all the people who can afford to pay, it's a big company like that. My father always paid his bills early— every single little bill. Even the small ones that didn't seem like they mattered, because he knew that those small bills paid kept small businesses running—"

"So you're comparing the big business with your father, and I'm a little business, just struggling to keep myself afloat," he said, his gaze locking on to hers. She knew that tone—she'd offended him again.

"Amos, I'm not the one who said you needed that

payment," she said. "And now you have it. I thought you'd be happy."

"It's how you see me, Miriam," he said. "It's how you've always seen me. I'm not some man struggling to begin. I'm respected in this community, you know. Well respected."

"*Yah*, I know!" She turned away, irritated, then turned back. "I'm not insulting your position in the community, Amos. I'm not suggesting that you're unable to run your own business. But I do think you could do with a little more respect from the Englisher businesses you sell to. How many of them have short-paid you? How many have expected deep discounts in order to do business with you again? *They* don't respect you nearly enough!"

"Let me ask you this," Amos said, his gaze narrowing. "How many businesses have you actually run all by yourself?"

She blinked at him. "My father owned—"

"I'm not asking about your father," he said. "You. How many have you owned and operated, making all the decisions yourself, accepting any consequence that came from them on your own shoulders without any hope of someone bailing you out? How many?"

Was he trying to embarrass her now? She felt the blood drain from her face, and she pressed her lips together. This was why they'd always fought. Because he couldn't see when she was helping! He refused to see when she was right!

"You think watching my father run a veritable empire taught me nothing?" she asked curtly.

"I think watching something done and doing it yourself are two very different experiences," he replied. "And until you've run your own business, you have no right to give advice as if you were your father. You aren't Leroy Schwartz. He might have taught you, but he didn't put those businesses into your hands."

Because her father had never intended for her to run them—that was the thought that was running through Miriam's mind, and it settled like a rock in her chest. Her *daet* hadn't left her even one business to run on her own. He'd given everything to Japheth, even after ten years of her working tirelessly by his side. He'd never given her the chance to prove herself.

Miriam felt her chin tremble with emotion, and she looked up to see *Mammi*'s friend Doris standing in the doorway to the kitchen. She must have come through the front door, and they hadn't heard her.

Amos's ears turned red, and they both instinctively angled away from each other.

"I just wanted to let you know that I'm heading back home to start my own dinner," Doris said, glancing between them. "I don't want to leave Mary alone out there. She needs help to come back inside."

"Thank you for telling us," Amos said. "I'm sorry about—" He glanced toward Miriam. "We, uh, we were just having a discussion. Everything is fine."

"Hmm." Doris raised an eyebrow, and Miriam felt the judgment. This time, it might be deserved. *Mammi* needed a supportive and loving environment, not two people who fought like a couple of magpies.

"I'll go help her inside," Amos said, and he headed back through the house toward the front door with Doris on his heels.

Miriam stood there for a moment, her heart pounding in her chest. Amos always had known how to cast a barb that hurt. He didn't even know he was doing it, because she'd never told him how deeply her father's choices had stung her. He was doing what he did best—making a point.

She turned toward the table and saw the bakery box sitting there. She moved toward it, and plucked the lid open. Inside there were three plump, chocolate whoopee pies with white, whipped centers.

Tears welled in her eyes. Whoopee pies. Had he remembered that first meal alone together, a pot of tea between them and a box of whoopee pies? She looked in the direction Amos had gone, and there was the sound of the front screen door slamming shut and the murmur of voices outside.

She shut the lid to the bakery box.

Amos had probably forgotten that little detail about their history. Because if Amos had any fond memories at all of their brief time together, they hadn't softened him one bit.

Chapter Six

Mammi sat in a rocking chair on the porch, her hands folded in her lap. She had a blanket over her legs despite the warm weather, and she looked up as Amos came outside and gave him a gentle smile. Jeremiah Miller, the boy mowing the grass, had finished his work and he waved as he headed back up the drive. Amos had hired the boy to do the mowing for a set amount each month, and so far, he'd been doing a good job.

"Doris said you're ready to come in," Amos said to his grandmother. "It was nice that she came by."

"Yah, I was glad to see her. I treasure these times now even more than I did before. But I'm not quite ready to come yet," she said. "Why don't you sit?"

The only other place to sit was the swing, and Amos settled onto it, leaning forward onto his elbows to keep himself stationary.

"It's a lovely evening," Amos said.

"Yah," she agreed. "How did things go with that big order?"

"Uh—" He wasn't sure how much his grandmother

had overheard from inside. "It went well. They paid in full."

Mammi smiled. "So your wife was of some use."

Amos nodded and gave his grandmother a rueful look. "*Yah*, *Mammi*, she was."

"Did you tell her that?" *Mammi* raised her eyebrows.

"I—" Had he said it in so many words? "I told her that they paid."

"That didn't sound like a grateful spirit inside there," *Mammi* said.

So she had heard. He felt his face heat. "Did you all hear that?"

"*Yah*, I'm afraid we did," *Mammi* said softly. "I won't lie to you, Amos."

Amos scrubbed a hand over his beard and looked in the direction that Jeremiah Miller had gone. The boy looked over his shoulder, then picked up his pace. Amos felt a wash of shame. He had no business arguing with Miriam like that—even if she saw him as beneath her. What must young Jeremiah think? And very soon the Millers would be discussing what happened here today.

"I'm sorry about that, *Mammi*. Miriam and I—" He cleared his throat.

"You know how to pluck each other's last nerves," *Mammi* said. "I know, dear. I don't mean to make this harder on you. You are a calm and sweet man, and Miriam might be the only woman capable of getting a rise out of you."

"She might be," he agreed, and he looked at his grandmother in misery. "What do I do with her?"

"You might get further if you stopped insulting her late father," *Mammi* said frankly.

"I'm not insulting him—" Amos started.

"You are," she said. "Leroy Schwartz may have been a difficult man, and I know that he did nothing to help you and your wife reconcile. He was proud—forgive me for pointing it out—but he was also her *daet*. And she isn't going to see his faults, especially now. How do you think it helps to point out the things that hurt her most?"

Amos sighed. He had every reason to resent her late father. Leroy had been obstinate and had encouraged his daughter to stay away from her marital home. He'd expected Amos to somehow raise himself up to a higher level to be worthy of Leroy's youngest, his much-loved daughter. Leroy had set impossible standards for Amos to achieve in order to gain his respect, and that had left Amos angry and resistant. But that adored daughter would see her father differently.

"Your *mamm* and *daet* struggled to get along, too," *Mammi* said. "Your *daet* was not a gentle man. But you aren't like him—"

"And Miriam isn't like my *mamm*, either," he countered.

"No, she isn't," *Mammi* agreed. "Still, growing up you didn't have a good example of a happy marriage at home. I don't know why your *daet* was so hard on your *mamm*. Your grandfather had many a stern discussion with him about it, too, I can promise you. It wasn't right, Amos."

"I know that," he said, feeling a rise of defensiveness. "I know that better than anyone. Do you think I want to end up like my parents?"

"Of course not," *Mammi* sighed. "May I give you some advice, Amos?"

"It couldn't hurt," he replied, his voice tight.

The last thing he wanted was to end up like his father. His father was the one who made their home so nervous and unhappy—he'd been clear on that all this time.

"Be the change you want to see in your relationships," *Mammi* said softly. "It feels ever so justified to point out where someone else is going wrong, but dear boy, you have to look at the plank of wood in your own eye first. And we all have one. So treat your wife with the consideration you would like her to give you." *Mammi* smoothed her hand over the blanket on her lap. "I was married for a good many years, Amos. I know that it works."

"Was *Dawdie* ever difficult?" Amos asked. "Like my *daet* was?"

"Sometimes, but not for long," she said, and she smiled over at him. "In a long marriage, people learn how to bring out the best in each other. We're all capable of sinking to our worst, Amos. But with a husband and wife, they have to learn how to find the best in the other and draw it out. Because we're all capable of goodness, too. And maybe we need to be willing to let someone draw out the best in us, too, or you just get caught in a stubborn circle. That was a lesson in life that your *daet* never took to heart."

And maybe that was the secret to the next few weeks. Amos needed to change his approach to Miriam. He needed to be a better man.

"I'll try, *Mammi*," he said. "Thank you for the advice."

Mammi smiled and held out her hand. "Help me up. We should go inside now."

Amos rose to his feet and took his grandmother's frail hand. He steadied her as she stood up, and put an arm around her to help support her weight.

"The food smells wonderful," *Mammi* said. "Miriam has worked hard. Don't forget to acknowledge that."

"I won't forget, *Mammi*," he said with a faint smile.

Mammi ate very little at dinner, but she beamed in appreciation of the whoopee pie for dessert. She took a small bite and nodded her thanks, but she didn't eat much more than that.

"I'm ready to take my medication and go bed now," *Mammi* said. "I hope you two don't mind."

Miriam helped *Mammi* to change, and then Amos lifted her into bed. He sat on the edge and read some of her favorite passage from the Bible while her eyes drifted shut.

"'The Lord is my shepherd; I shall not want. He maketh me to lie down in green pastures: he leadeth me beside the still waters. He restoreth my soul: he leadeth me in the paths of righteousness for his name's sake—'" He paused and looked down at his grandmother's slow breathing. She was asleep, but this next verse was for his own comfort. "'Yea, though I walk through the valley of the shadow of death, I will fear no evil: for thou art with me; thy rod and thy staff they comfort me...'"

Mammi looked peaceful in her slumber, and he closed the Bible and put it down on the bed next to her.

Gott, be with my grandmother, he prayed, and he rose to his feet and headed out of the front room, now dim with the shut curtains, and went through the hall-way to the kitchen. All was silent and still. The dishes were done, the table cleaned off and the scent of dinner still hung in the air. He spotted the open bakery box on the end of the table—there was one whoopee pie left.

Amos closed the box and carried it with him outside. *Mammi* had been right—he needed a better start with Miriam this time around. These few weeks together didn't have to be misery. They could respect each other, and maybe Miriam felt disrespected by him, too.

He let the side screen door clatter shut behind him, and as he walked around the side of the house, he saw the chains of the porch swing moving back and forth before he spotted Miriam behind a veil of lilac bushes.

Had she come out here to avoid him? And if she had, did he blame her?

Amos cleared his throat as he came around to the front of the house, and Miriam stopped swinging.

"There's a whoopee pie left," he said, holding up the box.

"You go ahead," Miriam said. "I don't mind."

"Do you want to share it?" he asked.

Miriam's cheeks pinked. "It's okay, Amos. You don't have to smooth things over with me."

"I think I do," he countered. "I haven't been entirely fair to you. *Mammi* pointed that out, for the record. And she was right. I'm being hard on you for things you had no control over."

Amos came up the steps and Miriam moved over on the swing.

"If you come with dessert, you can sit," she said with a small smile.

Amos sat down next to her and they resumed the slow swinging. He opened the box and held it out to her. Miriam broke off a piece of the whoopee pie and, using one hand to catch crumbs, she took a bite.

Amos did the same—and finally the dessert felt like the treat it was supposed to be.

"I was being sensitive," Miriam said quietly. "My *daet* didn't leave me anything to run. You don't know how that feels. He left it all to Japheth, and left me nothing. After working with him more closely than my brother did!"

"Really?" Amos looked over at her. "I thought Japheth—"

"Oh, *Daet* let him oversee a few businesses himself," Miriam said. "So I guess there is that. But I was the one who was at *Daet*'s side. I went with him when he checked on his management, and I went over financial statements with him, and double-checked numbers from the bank. I was the one listening to all of *Daet*'s advice. I was there."

"I didn't mean to rub that in," Amos said.

"I know…" She took another bite. "But I'm sensitive about it, all the same."

Amos nudged her arm with his. "I'm sorry he did that."

"Thank you." She took another small bite.

"Do you remember that first meal we had when we got married?" he asked.

Miriam's gaze flickered up to meet his. "I thought you'd forgotten."

"Of course not," he said. "Whoopee pies were your favorite, and I wanted to make you happy. That's why

I bought them this time—you and *Mammi* both love them and I hoped that it would… I don't know…make us all feel some happiness."

"It was thoughtful," Miriam said. "I had a tough day today."

"You had a victory today," he replied. "I should have thanked you properly for your help with that big order. You were right about them. If I'd done it my way, I would have lost money. So thank you."

Miriam smiled. "You're welcome. Am I allowed to mention that my *daet* taught me that?"

"You already did mention it earlier, and I'd rather not get into it again," he said, and he laughed softly. "Miriam, you can take the credit for having seen a situation that needed a different approach. That was you."

Miriam nodded. "I know you didn't get along with him, Amos, but I miss him. He might have been gruff and ornery, but never to me. He was always kindness and patience with *me*."

Even old Leroy could be softened by his youngest daughter, it seemed.

"It must still be a very fresh grief," he said softly.

"*Yah*. Very fresh," she whispered.

"I'm so sorry for all you lost when your *daet* died," Amos said. "I know how you loved him."

Miriam's chin trembled and she looked away to hide her emotion, but she didn't need to do that with him. He was her husband, after all, and if she couldn't cry over her father's death here, then where could she do it?

Amos reached out and took Miriam's hand in his. He ran his thumb over the tops of her fingers and then gave her hand a gentle squeeze. She squeezed his hand in return.

"No one loves you quite like your *daet* does," Miriam said, her voice thick with emotion. "I feel almost… orphaned." She pulled her hand back and wiped her cheeks with the palms of her hands.

Amos had lost his parents young, and that adrift feeling of not having a *mamm* and *daet* here in the land of the living to encourage him and be proud of him had never quite gone away. But he'd never had a warm relationship with his own father, so maybe he was envious that she'd had that.

"I know I'm not quite what you wanted, Miriam," he said. "I know our relationship isn't any kind of ideal, Amish or English. But I want to make things easier for you—for what I'm worth."

And he meant it. They might end up with a strange friendship forged over years of supporting each other from a distance, but he would always be her husband—for the rest of their lives.

Miriam took another bite of the whoopee pie, and the sweet cream mingled with chocolate cake. White paint flaked off the porch floor where her shoes touched, and she let her gaze move out to the freshly mown yard with the neat rows of grass clippings. She loved this scent— one she hadn't stopped to enjoy in far too long. She'd always been so busy with *Daet*.

It was strange to be swinging with Amos like this… almost like a regular married couple, enjoying a springtime evening after dinner. Maybe she'd spent so much time with *Daet* because she'd been able to avoid seeing other happily married couples, like Japheth and his wife, Arleta. Being with *Daet* let her forget what she was missing out on, because he'd always been peculiar, and he'd never remarried.

"You can have the rest," Miriam said, nudging the box in Amos's direction. He took the last piece of whoopee pie, and for a moment, they ate in silence.

"There has to be a way for us to be happy," Amos said.

She shot him a wary look.

"Not living together," he clarified. "I mean… No one else is going to understand our arrangement, but there has to be a way that we can be friendly toward each other and both live the life that gives us the most contentment."

"So what would be different than what we've been doing the last ten years?" she asked.

"Maybe we could…stay in touch?" He looked over at her. "Write letters. Visit from time to time. I do wish you well. I wouldn't mind seeing your strip mall in Edson one day."

Did he mean it? Sitting here with him on this swing, it almost felt possible that they could have some sort of workable relationship that kept them friendly.

"Maybe we could try that," she said.

"I don't want to see you unhappy, Miriam," he said quietly. "Especially not because of me."

"I'm okay, Amos—"

"No, it's more than that," he said. "I never told you much about my *daet* because he didn't match up to yours…at all."

"Oh?" She felt her breath catch. It was true, he'd

never spoken much about him. But he'd passed away when Amos was a boy, and she'd assumed that was the reason.

"My *daet* believed that the Bible was the answer for everything," he said.

"It is," Miriam said frankly.

"But the Bible doesn't mention every single thing that a person might encounter," Amos said. "There might be situations where we have to extrapolate an answer from the Bible. My *mamm* was depressed. I don't mean she felt blue or a little moody sometimes. I mean that she struggled with feelings so miserable that she would take to her bed for a week at a time." He licked his lips and glanced over at her. "One winter, when she was in one of her bad stretches, she wandered out into a snowstorm, and she would have frozen to death out there if *Daet* hadn't gone after her."

The thought chilled her, and they stopped rocking. He'd held all of this inside?

"You were embarrassed to tell me?" she asked.

"*Mamm* and *Daet* were already gone," he said. "And quite frankly, I didn't want to give you anything more to look down on than you already had."

Miriam blinked at him. "Amos, I wouldn't have looked down on you."

"You already did," he said. "But I don't want to argue about that. The point is, my *mamm* suffered from depression, and after that snowstorm my *daet* brought her to a doctor. The doctor prescribed some medication, and when *Mamm* took it, she felt a lot better. She was more like herself. She'd get up and cook meals and talk to us about our days at school. She'd mend our clothes, and plan for the weekends."

"So, it helped," Miriam said.

"It did," he said. "The problem was, my *daet* didn't like the idea of the medication. He said if taking some pills made her act normally, then she could act normally without them. He said she should pray more and try harder. So he took the pills away."

Miriam frowned. "That sounds cruel. If a doctor said—"

"We don't agree with everything an Englisher doctor says," he said. "And *Daet* drew a line. I often thought it was the expense—they had to pay for every bottle of them, and if *Mamm* needed them daily, well, that would add up. Anyway, *Mamm* stayed off her medication for a long time. She struggled through her sad times, and she did her best to keep taking care of us when she was so unhappy that I was afraid she'd go walking out into a storm again. But I'd seen what life could be like when she took those pills, and it was wonderful! It was happy in our home again… But *Daet* wouldn't allow her to do the one thing that would make her happy."

Amos looked over at Miriam, sadness swimming in his dark gaze.

"Oh, Amos…" she murmured.

"I promised myself I'd never do that to a woman," he said softly. "I told myself that I'd never stand between my wife and happiness."

Miriam's breath caught. "You don't!"

"I'm glad. I want you to be happy, Miriam. And even if what it takes to make you happy goes against my view of what ought to be, or how things ought to work, I won't stand in your way."

Miriam felt a welling of sympathy for her estranged husband. There was so much he'd never told her...so much she'd never even imagined lay beneath the surface. She slipped her hand into his warm, calloused grip.

"I appreciate that, Amos," she said.

His hand tightened around hers, and they started to swing again, back and forth, his strong hand moving gently over her fingers. He was a handsome man, and sitting here holding his hand, she could imagine so much more between them... But that would be selfish of her. She knew her true personality, and she knew how little Amos wanted her meddling in his carpentry shop. Some respect and sympathy between them didn't change who they were at heart.

In a way, it was easier to resent him than to respect him, because then she had to admit how much she was missing out on with this marriage—how much she was letting go. What must the other women in the community, like Fannie, think of her now?

"Are people talking about us?" she asked.

"A few," Amos replied.

She nodded. "I saw Fannie Mast on the way home today."

"Oh?" He looked over at her. "You two used to be good friends."

"Sometimes I think that *Gott* might be trying to teach me some humility, Amos," she said quietly. "Of all the things I was proud of, *Gott* has stripped them away. I was proud of my family, and my *daet* is dead. I was proud of our businesses and our ability to grow them successfully, and they have all been left to my brother if I don't find those papers. And once, years ago when I was young and idealistic, I was proud to have a husband."

"You still have a husband," he said.

She smiled at him faintly. "In our way, I suppose. But not in the way anyone else would approve of. Fannie used to fight with Silas so bitterly. Did you know that?"

Amos shook his head. "No. They seem so happy—"

"It's private, so you can't say anything. This is a secret I'm telling you as my husband. She did the same with Silas," she said. She knew Amos well enough to know that she could trust his discretion.

"Okay…"

"Apparently, they are happy now," she said. "But when they first got married, they were like anyone else and they had to adjust to married life. Silas wasn't very affectionate. He expected Fannie to do her duty, put the meals on the table, to clean the house and take care of the garden, and he never once thanked her for any of it. She was…" Miriam thought back to the young, newly married Fannie. "She was very sensitive, and kindhearted, and hopeful."

"What improved things for them?" Amos asked.

"I left." Miriam looked over at him.

"No…" Amos shook his head.

"I'm serious," she replied. "I was a wake-up for them. I used to encourage her to tell Silas how she felt, and to stand up to him. He could be such a bully…"

"And when you left, it scared them, seeing what could have happened to them if they carried on that way," Amos said.

"I think so," Miriam replied. "That, and she no longer had me there to encourage her to revolt."

"Did you?" he asked.

She felt some heat in her cheeks. "A little."

Amos chuckled softly. "No harm done. They're fine now. They have all those *kinner*, and seem very happy when I see them on Service Sunday. Silas and I get along quite well."

"Is he…nice?" Miriam asked. "He didn't seem very nice to Fannie back then. Is he kind? Does he respect her?"

"Yah," Amos said. "He loves her dearly, Miriam. He talks about her all the time. Fannie's baking, Fannie's singing, Fannie's garden… You'd think there was only one woman on the earth."

So Silas *had* loved her… Was it possible that Miriam had been stirring up trouble for that couple when what Fannie had needed was a little encouragement? If so, she hadn't meant to, and she felt truly sorry for it now. Back then, she'd thought that most women must be just like her—chafing at the restraints, eager to do more than women's work or run a small shop, to wrap her brain around some new challenge that could really excite her. But that didn't seem to be true. Most women in their communities loved their time at home, their time with their *kinner*, evenings quilting with friends…

Other women were content.

"I was foolish back then," Miriam said quietly. "And Fannie now knows it."

"How so?" Amos asked.

"I thought that Fannie was just like I was," Miriam said. "I thought she just wasn't strong enough to stand

up to her husband and tell him what she really needed.
I used to encourage her to have it out with Silas, to tell
him what she really thought of how he acted toward
her. I thought she deserved better treatment. Maybe the
one she wasn't strong enough to stand up to was me."

Amos was silent, but he cast her a sad look. Her
strong personality had always been her biggest weakness, and there was no getting around it. It was what
had kept her single in Edson, too.

"It doesn't matter now," Miriam said, and she pulled
her hand back from his warm, comforting clasp.

"You weren't the terrifying storm you seem to
think," he said quietly.

"No?" she said. "Then why didn't anyone come after
me to talk me into coming back?"

There hadn't been any women coming by to talk to
her about forgiveness or to give her advice about making up with her husband. There hadn't been any visits
from elders and their wives to give some advice to a
woman who'd run away from her husband.

"Because your father was particularly imposing,"
Amos replied, but he smiled as he said the words, taking the sting out of them.

"That's true," she admitted ruefully.

Her *daet* had certainly had a way about him. He
could use a single look to cow an Englisher businessman trying to drive down a fair price. And he'd used
that look in protection of his daughter.

"Miriam, you were nothing like I expected," Amos
said. "But we're okay. We're both living happy lives.
I've got Noah and Thomas, who treat me like family,

and *Gott* has been good to me. I feel blessed with the life I lead. I really do."

Miriam looked over at him—the calm, content man she'd married. And she was so far from content, so far from happy with how her life had turned out. But if she'd learned something on this trip back to Redemption, it was that her own frustration couldn't be put onto others.

Her husband had built a happy life without her, and she couldn't upset another life just because she felt unsettled and not quite fulfilled.

"I'm glad," Miriam said. "I'm going to take a walk, I think. I could use a little time alone."

Amos nodded. "Sure. Thank you for sharing the whoopee pie with me."

They stopped swinging and Miriam stood up. She needed to walk and pray, and see if she could find a portion of that trusting contentment that her husband had found. If *Gott* could give Amos that kind of peace, maybe He would grant it to her, too.

Chapter Seven

The next morning, Amos went out early to gather eggs from the chicken coop and then muck out the stables where their three horses were housed. The air was cool, and dew hung heavy on the grass and the small, barely sprouting garden plants. He paused at the outside row of pea plants and touched the coiling springs.

He glanced back toward the house. There was a light on in the kitchen, and he saw Miriam pass in front of a window, her arms full of wood for the stove. He stood there, motionless, letting the moment wash over him.

His wife was home.

It felt strange…uncomfortably good. He couldn't get used to this obviously. She wasn't staying. But *Mammi* had been right that some help around here while she was so sick was incredibly welcome. Just recently, the outdoor chores as well as the cooking and what he could manage of the cleaning had fallen to him. *Mammi*'s health had started failing rather abruptly.

The sun was peeking over the horizon, glowing pink in the mist that hung over the fields. Mornings like this one had always made him feel closer to *Gott*. He'd often thought about the fact that *Gott* had given them sunrises and sunsets. He could just as easily have created a world where the sun came up and went down with the same regularity and no fanfare. But *Gott* splashed the sky in color twice a day.

And that same *Gott*, the one who loved them enough to give them beauty for the sake of beauty and did not make mistakes, was going to bring *Mammi* home one day soon. Amos trusted *Gott*, but that didn't stop his heart from breaking. *Mammi* had been a beautiful spot in his life. She was like a splash of sunrise.

The rumble of an engine drew Amos's attention, and he walked toward the drive to see a pickup truck coming up to the house. He knew the vehicle well—this was Wollie Zook.

"Good morning!" Amos called as he sauntered toward the truck.

Wollie turned off the engine and hopped out. He was dressed in Amish clothes, which looked odd coming out of the driver's side of a vehicle.

"Good morning, Amos," Wollie said.

"How are things going?" Amos asked. Wollie wasn't coming by for a chat, he was pretty sure. There was something wrong.

"I didn't want to disturb you all, but I've got a problem over at my place that I need a hand with."

"Oh?" Amos said. "What's wrong?"

"It's an axle on my buggy," Wollie said. "It got knocked out of alignment going over a pothole, and I can see the problem, but I need a hand fixing it."

"Is that why you're back driving the truck?" Amos asked.

Wollie's face colored a little. "*Yah*, well… I didn't have a lot of time. I wanted to come find you before I headed to work, and…"

Some conveniences were hard to let go of. If Wollie were living a fully Amish life, he'd have walked to his nearest neighbor, not driven to his neighbor of choice.

"It's okay," Amos said with a shake of his head. "I can help you out. How much time do you have before you leave for work?"

"About three hours," Wollie said. "My shift doesn't start until ten."

"I can help you this morning. Noah and Thomas have keys to the shop—I can be a little late," Amos said.

"That would be great," Wollie said. "Thank you."

"For sure." Amos nodded again, and he eyed the younger man. "It's not easy, is it?"

"Coming back Amish?" Wollie let out a breath. "It's supposed to be easy for me—I was born to this life. But it's not as easy as I thought. I got used to things—Englisher conveniences that just saved time. Like the truck. I told myself I wouldn't drive it again, but I kept it, just in case of emergency. I've got four *kinner*, after all, and Natasha is expecting again. We haven't told anyone yet, so don't tell people, if you don't mind."

"Congratulations," Amos said. "That's great news."

"Thank you," Wollie said. "But all my other *kinner* were born English, and…things can go wrong. I'm feeling cautious."

"*Yah*, I know," Amos said.

Wollie pursed his lips. "It's not easy for Natasha,

either. She's been trying to use the woodstove that we had installed a couple of months ago, and she's having trouble with it—burns just about everything she cooks. As for sewing—my *mamm* is still sewing my shirts for me, because it's too much to ask Natasha to do." Wollie dropped his gaze. "I've started to wonder if I was wrong to ask her to live an Amish life with me."

"Wollie, you married an Englisher woman who was willing to try to be Amish with you. That's something extraordinary right there," Amos said seriously.

"True, that isn't common, is it?" Wollie's gaze flickered toward the house. "Your wife is back, isn't she?"

"*Yah*, for a little while," Amos said.

"Not for good?" Wollie asked.

Amos sighed. "Our marriage is complicated. Be thankful for a wife who can live with you English or Amish. You are a blessed man, Wollie."

Wollie smiled. "*Yah*, I am."

His smile faltered. He looked worried.

"Miriam isn't really a homemaker," Amos said. "So I don't think she'd be the right one to teach your wife how to keep an Amish home."

"I think she needs a friendly face, more than anything," Wollie said.

Miriam had a soft spot in her heart for struggling wives, it seemed. "Maybe she'll be willing to show her some basics. I mean, she's a good cook…"

"Do you think she might?" Wollie said. "I think my wife would appreciate the social contact. She's so frustrated."

"I can ask," Amos said, and felt a sudden wave of misgiving. Volunteering Miriam for something she didn't want to do would only cause more friction between them. He was overstepping; he could feel it. But the words were already out.

"Tell you what," Amos said. "Let me finish up here, and I'll come by your place. If she can help, I'll let you know."

Wollie smiled and bounced the truck keys in his palm. "Thank you, Amos. I'll see you later on, then."

Amos watched as Wollie pulled his truck around and headed back up the drive. He glanced toward the house. Wollie might have the challenge of trying to reintegrate his family into an Amish way of life, but at least he had a wife dedicated to staying by his side. Amos had a wife home with him for a little while longer, but there was an unrooted, unsettled feeling to this arrangement, and he envied Wollie just a little bit.

Amos headed up the steps, and when he went inside the house and washed his hands, he saw Miriam cranking the windows open to catch the morning cross breezes. A pot of oatmeal bubbled fragrantly on the stove, and *Mammi* was already settled in the easy chair.

"Was that Wollie Zook?" Mammi asked.

"*Yah*, that was him," Amos replied. He went over to where his grandmother sat and kissed her on the cheek. "How did you sleep, *Mammi*?"

"Oh, as well as I seem to sleep these days," *Mammi* said.

"What does that mean?" he asked.

"I wake up a lot," she replied. "But nighttime is a good time for prayer, Amos. When you can lie in the darkness and seek the Lord."

"Were you in pain?" he asked.

"The medication helps with that," she replied. "No need to fuss over me, dear boy."

He'd always be a "dear boy" in *Mammi*'s eyes, and the endearment brought a lump to his throat. He nodded and turned toward the kitchen.

"Wollie needs a hand fixing his buggy," Amos said. "That's why he drove the truck."

Miriam looked up from the biscuits she was cutting out on the floured counter. "A truck?"

"I know how it looks," Amos replied. "Wollie left the community to marry an Englisher woman. They had a bad fire and started reconnecting with us again, and they've decided to try to live an Amish life. The problem is, his wife is Englisher, and she doesn't see things the same way."

"She's a good Christian," *Mammi* said quietly.

Amos looked back at his grandmother.

"She is," *Mammi* said. "I saw her at the grocery store once, and she was in line to pay with her *kinner* all in the cart, and talking and reaching for things, and..." *Mammi* shook her head. "But there was this woman ahead of her in line who didn't have enough money to pay for her whole order, and she was going to start taking things out—things like milk and bread and meat. Things that would properly feed a family. And even though the Zooks lost so much in that fire, Natasha Zook handed the woman enough cash to cover her bill. Just handed it over. And when the woman said she'd pay her back, Natasha said not to worry about it. Just like that. And then she paid for her own order, and do you know? She had to put a few of her own things back because she didn't have enough. Some of the treats for the *kinner*."

Amos stood there in silence. He hadn't heard about that, and the thought of the good she'd done to that other woman, even though it meant she wouldn't have enough for her own grocery bill, was moving. That was the kind of Christian love that their Amish community tried to show.

"She's a good woman," *Mammi* said firmly. "And she's trying hard."

"It sounds like it," Miriam said quietly.

"Wollie mentioned that, uh—" Amos cleared his throat. "He mentioned how frustrated Natasha is right now. She grew up English, so doing things our way is hard for her. Cooking on a woodstove is a real challenge, and so is sewing. She's also lonely. I think she feels isolated. I—" He winced. "I know this is out of line for me to do, but I suggested that you might have enough time to help her—maybe just be friendly."

Miriam pressed her lips together. "I've got to be here with *Mammi*."

"Have her come here," *Mammi* said. "Sometimes all the help a woman needs is a little kindness. Tell her to come visit us today, and we'll show her how to do some basic sewing."

Amos looked over at Miriam. "Is that okay?"

"Yah." She nodded. "I'd be happy to show her a few things."

Miriam went over to the stove and stirred the pot of oatmeal a few times, then she pulled it off the heat and closed the damper on the stove. She moved with confidence around the kitchen, but he could see the sadness in her eyes.

Amos crossed the kitchen to keep his words with her private, and he lowered his voice.

"I'm sorry that I offered up your time like that," he said. "I knew it was too much the minute it came out of my mouth."

"It's okay." She shook her head and cast him a rueful smile.

"Having you here—" He swallowed searching inside of himself for the words. "It's been nice."

She looked at him, silent. He'd been expecting a joking comeback, or a roll of her eyes. Instead, she just looked at him.

"It's all too easy to fall into treating you like—" He dropped his gaze, not finishing.

"Like your actual wife?" she asked softly.

Amos looked up. *"Yah."*

Miriam picked up the pot with pot holders. "I am your wife, Amos. And until I leave, you can let me help you like a wife would do. If showing Natasha a few things will make things easier for you, I'm happy to do it."

She brushed past him with the hot pot of oatmeal toward the table, and he felt the old sadness come back. Miriam was being kind by helping out the way she was, but getting used to her presence, to this unnatural calm and peacefulness between them, wasn't good for him.

It would only hurt more when she left again.

"I'd better hurry up," he said. "I said I'd help Wollie with that axle, and then I have to get into work."

Sometimes it was better to focus on the day ahead instead of the hesitant, unrealistic hopes that had started inside of him.

* * *

Miriam had just finished pinning the last wet towel to the clothesline when a truck turned down the drive and came rumbling up to the house. Miriam recognized it from that morning—it was the Zooks' vehicle. A blonde woman in Amish garb was driving, and after she parked, she opened the door and got out. She looked hesitantly toward Miriam.

"Hello!" Miriam called, and she headed down the steps toward her. "You must be Natasha. I'm Miriam Lapp."

"Hello." Natasha glanced over her shoulder as her children came tumbling out the back seat of the truck. They were all dressed in Amish clothing, as well— two boys and two little girls, all beneath the age of ten.

"Welcome," Miriam said with a smile. The children smiled back, but hung close to their mother. Natasha tucked a stray tendril of hair behind her ear.

"Your husband is helping mine repair that buggy," Natasha said. "Thank you for that. Wollie's determined to take it to work today."

"He's happy to help," Miriam said. "I'm glad you made it."

"Me, too," she replied with a smile.

"Have you ever played horseshoes?" Miriam asked the kids.

"Our *daet* showed us how," the older boy said.

Daet. She noticed that he'd used the Pennsylvania Dutch word. She smiled at that. *Kinner* could adjust quickly to changes, and moving to a life of farming and outdoor activities would be an adventure for them—at least during the summer.

"If I got you the game, could you set it up?" Miriam asked.

"*Yah*, I can do it," the boy said in Dutch.

"That was very good!" Miriam said. "Nicely done."

"My *mammi* taught me that," he said, switching back to English. "I can say a few things."

"All right, tell me another thing you can say in Dutch..."

It didn't take long to get the *kinner* enjoying some outdoor play, and Miriam led Natasha inside where *Mammi* was dozing in her easy chair. They could see the *kinner* out the window, tossing horseshoes and laughing. The smallest girl lay next to the garden, and she was pushing little rocks into the soil as if she was planting.

"Oh, I'm sorry—" Natasha started toward the window.

"She's fine," Miriam said. "It's how they learn. She's not hurting anything."

Natasha smiled shakily. "This is very nice of you to have us over like this. I appreciate it."

"Have you started learning to drive a buggy yet?" Miriam asked.

"I'm afraid of the horses," Natasha said. "I almost got kicked once, and I haven't learned how to hitch up. Besides, we only have one buggy right now, and my husband needed it for work. But honestly, even if we had another one, I'm not sure I could manage driving it."

Miriam nodded. "There are a lot of changes to get used to."

"I'm not doing terribly well, to be honest. The kids know more Dutch than I do at this point, and I burn everything I cook." She laughed uncomfortably.

"Sit down," Miriam said. "Let me get some cookies."

She brought a plate of shortbread cookies to the table and sat down opposite the other woman.

"Can I ask you something?" Miriam said.

"Sure," Natasha replied.

"Why are you doing this?" Miriam asked. "Don't get me wrong—everyone is so happy that you are. You're very, very welcome in this community, and I've been told that your husband's parents are overjoyed to have you all come to the Amish faith together…" Miriam leaned forward. "But why did *you* choose this life?"

"For him," Natasha said with a weak shrug.

"How is your family taking it?" Miriam asked. "Your parents and siblings, I mean. They're English, I take it?"

"Yes, they're… English." Natasha smiled faintly. "And they aren't taking it well. They think we're crazy and my parents are worried about the kids getting enough schooling, and having a future, and…" She sighed. "So, it has been tense with them."

"And you did all this for Wollie?" Miriam asked.

Natasha was silent for a moment. "I met Wollie at a baseball game. The Amish young people were playing against our church's youth group, and Wollie and I started talking, and…it all just came together. I think we fell in love that very day. We talked for hours, and he was just the kindest, gentlest man I'd ever met. And when he looked at me, I could see exactly how he felt about me, and I'd never experienced that before."

Miriam held her breath. Neither had she, for that matter…

"And you decided to get married?" she asked.

"Not right away. We started seeing each other. He

came with me to some church events, and we'd go out for drives together in the car. Once he brought the buggy, but we drew a lot of attention with the buggy, so we stopped that." Natasha glanced toward *Mammi*, whose eyes were still closed. "We got married because we loved each other too much not to get married. I truly believe that God created us for each other, and I could see how He'd brought us together. Back then, his parents had wanted him to marry a strict Amish girl, and I wouldn't have been acceptable, anyway. And my parents were very happy to show Wollie the English way of living, so we went to where there was more support. Being together was what mattered most to us."

Miriam nodded. "I do understand that. Your family was more supportive of the marriage... That makes sense. But now?"

"Coming back to the Amish faith is for Wollie," Natasha said. "I hadn't realized how much he'd given up by turning his back on the Amish culture. Over the years we talked more about why you all do what you do, and I saw the beauty in it. Besides, I could see my husband's yearning for the way he was raised, and it was draining away a part of him to be away from this life. So when our home burned down, I agreed that the time might be right to learn how to live Amish." Natasha smiled, her face lighting up. "Do you believe in people being created for each other?"

Miriam didn't know how to answer, but thankfully Natasha didn't seem to require one.

"I believe that God created Wollie and me for each other, and that no other man could make me as happy as Wollie does," Natasha said. "And Wollie thinks the same thing. We do things together or not at all. That's how we do everything."

"You don't think there might have been other men you could have been compatible with?" Miriam asked.

"Compatible? Maybe…" Natasha took a bite of a cookie. "But there's a difference between being brought together by God's own hand and stumbling across someone you have compatibility with."

"I suppose…" Miriam sucked in a slow breath.

She hadn't experienced either… She and Amos weren't even compatible, it seemed.

"My problem," Natasha said. "My biggest problem, at least, is that I'm not like you Amish women. You're all so good with your hands, and smart when it comes to practical matters. You're good cooks, good seamstresses, you take care of animals, know how to hang laundry!" She gestured out the window toward the fluttering towels on the line. "And all my life, I've never been good at those things. I've had other talents."

"Like what?" Miriam asked.

"I'm artistic," Natasha said. "I'm good at painting and drawing. I'm good at handling money—which I suppose is useful anywhere. I'm actually quite good with computers and gadgets, too. But that's no help here, is it? I'm just different."

Miriam nodded. "Me, too."

"What?" Natasha looked sincerely surprised.

"I'm very good with numbers and business," Miriam said. "I'm different, too."

"But you seem so—" Natasha glanced around the kitchen "—competent."

"I am." Miriam chuckled. "Natasha, can I tell you something?"

"Please!" the other woman said.

"We're not perfect and we're not all the same. Being Amish means believing in the same faith and the same values," Miriam said. "You don't have to be the same. You will be you, and you'll bring your strengths to the community, and you'll contribute. Maybe not with computers and the like, but you'll find a way to pitch in."

"But the canning, and pickling, and sewing, and gardening, and..." Natasha's voice trailed away.

"You'll learn," Miriam said with a shrug. "And maybe you'll never be terribly good at those things. But you'll find your place. You'll see. Don't put so much pressure on yourself."

Natasha's expression relaxed. "You're the first person to tell me that."

"Am I?" Miriam asked. "I'm sure I won't be the last."

"Since I'm here," Natasha said. "I'm having trouble cooking on my woodstove. Could you walk me through how you do it? Wollie's mother has shown me all of this, and I feel so silly asking her again and again. If I could cook just one meal for my family without burning it, I'd feel like a success."

"Of course," Miriam said, pushing her chair back. "Come—I'll show you some tricks."

An hour passed while Miriam showed Natasha how to cook with a woodstove, how to dampen the heat and how to get the perfect glow for baking bread. *Mammi* woke up from her nap and she gave a few tips of her own about how to run an Amish home.

And after the children had come inside for some pie

and tall glasses of milk, Natasha thanked Miriam for her kindness and sent the kids out to the truck, as it was time to go home for lunch.

"Thank you for taking the time for this," Natasha said earnestly. "I'm looking forward to starting the fire in my own stove for lunch. It'll be different this time, I'm sure."

"You're very welcome," Miriam said. "It was so nice to meet you."

When their guests had left, Miriam cast *Mammi* a tired smile.

"She's very nice," Miriam said. "I can see why her husband fell in love with her."

"*Yah*, I told you," *Mammi* said. "But I think you might have given her some bad advice."

Miriam shot the old woman a look of surprise. "What? When?"

"When you told her that she didn't need to worry about being like the other Amish women and that she could be different," *Mammi* said. "I woke up a few times there, and I was listening to you two talk… it was nice. But I don't think that advice was quite right."

"What would you have her do?" Miriam said with a shake of her head. "She can't change who she is! She'll have to find a way."

"She will," *Mammi* said softly. "But you're coming at this from a very different position than she is. She speaks very little of the language, knows very little about living an Amish life and knows very few people in our community. It's not going to be so simple for her."

Miriam was silent.

"You could be different because you've got Amish

pedigree all the way back to Switzerland," *Mammi* said. "No one will question how Amish you are. You might not like the life of an Amish wife, but you know the work because you've been taught it since you were tiny. And as for your affinity for business, it might be very useful if your husband will listen to your good instincts, but another woman wouldn't be able to do what you are doing and still be accepted. You come from a strongly Amish family and were raised by a wealthy Amish father who was revered in the community. It's different for you. You have some privilege and you get away with a whole lot more."

"I suppose it might be a little different," Miriam said after a moment.

"More than a little, dear," *Mammi* said frankly.

"If Natasha had a friend who could stand up for her—"

"But you aren't staying," *Mammi* said meekly. "So it can't be you."

Right. She was doing it again—dishing out advice that was in no way helpful to the woman who was looking to her for support. She rubbed her hands over her face.

"It's okay," *Mammi* said gently. "I think you encouraged her all the same. She has a mother-in-law to set her straight on the rest."

"I do try, *Mammi*," Miriam said with a sigh.

"I know," *Mammi* said with a tender smile. "And that's why I love you so."

Miriam went over to where the old woman sat and bent down, giving her a hug.

"I'm just going to go pick up the horseshoes," Miriam said. "I'll be right back."

As Miriam headed out into the noon sunlight, she felt another wave of regret—this one having nothing to do with Natasha or Fannie. This one was for her husband.

Miriam had expected more of Amos—it was true. She'd expected more growth in his business, and more strength in standing up to her father. But Amos didn't come from a family like hers, and her father was the kind of man who would not be moved once he'd made up his mind about something.

Miriam had expected Amos to be like her father— his business sense, his narrow focus, his effectiveness. But Amos wasn't her father. And he didn't have generations of accumulated land and businesses at his fingertips. He hadn't been raised by businessmen who'd taught him everything they knew.

Had Miriam's expectations of Amos…*her father's* expectations of him…been unfair?

Chapter Eight

Amos spent the first few hours of his day with Wollie, fixing that wagon axle. It took longer than they thought, and it still wasn't completely finished by the time they called it quits for the morning. But Wollie could finish it on his own that evening. Amos dropped him off at his work and then had to head all the way back to Redemption Carpentry, which took more time still. But there was no helping it—these things happened sometimes. As he rode, his mind kept slipping back to that unfinished box he'd found in his bedroom closet—the one he'd been carving for his and Miriam's first anniversary.

He'd never finished it. When she left, it hardly seemed like a priority. He couldn't bring himself to throw it into the stove, either. So it had sat up there for the better part of a decade, simply collecting dust.

But if things were going to be different for him and Miriam now—if they were going to be friends of some sort—then he felt like the change in their relationship deserved to be acknowledged between them. Maybe it was time to finish carving that box and give it to her, after all.

Would that be too much? Would he make things weird between them? But somehow, leaving that small box unfinished felt wrong now, and he couldn't quite explain why. But he needed to do something about it.

Amos arrived at the workshop a little after noon, and Noah and Thomas both looked up at his arrival. He nodded to the men as he hung up his lunch satchel on a peg by the door and dropped his hat on top.

"You made it," Noah said. "Is everything okay at home?"

They were asking about *Mammi*. "Yah, yah…" Amos nodded. "*Mammi* is doing okay. Every day she seems a little more tired, but she's okay."

Noah straightened and brushed the wood dust from his forearms.

"Wollie came by this morning," Amos went on. "He needed help with a damaged axle on his buggy, so I dropped by his place to help him fix it. It took a lot longer than I thought—one thing after another seemed to go wrong. It's not quite finished, but Wollie can do the rest on his own. So I drove him to work, and he figures he can get a ride back with a coworker. That's why I'm late."

"How's he doing?" Thomas asked.

"Pretty well," Amos replied. "He's finding it harder than he thought to readjust to Amish life, though."

"*He* is?" Thomas said, surprised. "I understand it being difficult for his wife and *kinner*, but—"

"He got used to their ways," Amos replied. "Like

having a truck. He said they kept it for emergencies, and when the buggy broke, he came to find me in his truck."

The men exchanged looks. None of them had extra Englisher vehicles for hard times. Amos knew how to be Amish, and it wasn't by having backup plans that went against the *Ordnung*. Marriage was supposed to be the same—vows and a life together, no divorce, no separation, no backup plan. Maybe Amos wasn't much better than Wollie right now.

"Once you've jumped the fence, coming back isn't so easy, is it?" Noah said quietly.

"It will take more time, I suppose," Thomas said. "Our *mamm* found it hard coming back, too. It isn't just the rules and giving up the Englisher conveniences. It's the friendships that have changed, and the way the community sees you. Our *mamm* really struggled with that coming back. She still does, somewhat."

"Still?" Amos asked.

"Coming home again means facing judgment," Noah said, his voice low.

Amos's mind went back to sitting on the swing next to Miriam, her soft hand in his. Miriam was facing judgment—from friends, family, people who'd only ever heard about her and hadn't even met her. And she'd felt safe enough with him to open up about it…

Things were changing, and Miriam had started to trust him, of all people. He hadn't expected that.

"Amos?" Noah said.

Amos realized he'd been lost in thought, and he looked up. "Sorry, what?"

"The bank statement arrived with the mail today," Noah said. "It's on your desk in the office."

"Thanks. I'll go take a look."

Amos headed in the direction of his office while Thomas and Noah turned back to their work in shaping a sleigh bed. Their voices mingled with the swish of the planer, the scent of freshly cut wood accenting the air.

The office was just off the side of the showroom. It was a small room with a large, plain desk and a bank of filing cabinets. One long, narrow window let in a shaft of sunlight, illuminating a white envelope on his desk. That would be the bank statement.

Amos sat down at the desk and pulled out his ledgers. He kept careful track of his work, the payments, expected payments…and for the last couple of months, his accounts had been off. He kept hoping that they'd rectify themselves somehow before the next bank statement… He'd check again today.

Amos opened the envelope and cracked open his newest ledger. For the next few minutes he scoured the columns, looking for the missing money. He'd made a mistake somewhere, obviously, because there was no way that Noah or Thomas were stealing from him. Still, he needed to know where he'd gone wrong, and he went over the numbers carefully, cross-checking as he went.

Two hours passed that way, and when there was a tap on the door, he roused himself.

"Come in," he called.

Noah opened the door and looked inside. "Everything okay, Amos?"

"We're out about five hundred dollars," Amos said.

"Out?" Noah frowned.

"I've made a mistake somehow, and I don't know where." Amos straightened his shoulders and rolled his neck. "I might just have to write it off and we'll carry on."

"You could ask Miriam," Noah said.

Amos eyed the younger man for a moment. "I did ask her to help me out a bit while she's here..."

"Well, then?" Noah said.

Amos sighed. It was the tally of numbers that held him back... If she never knew the actual amount of money that moved through his business, then he could let her believe he was more successful than he was. If he opened his books to her, then there would be no more room for inflated assumptions.

"It's my own pride," Amos said quietly. "Her father was a wealthy man, and this business would have been small potatoes for him...and for her."

"You aren't ashamed of a successfully run carpentry shop!" Noah said.

"No, I'm not." Amos shook his head. "And she did offer to help, so I'll ask Miriam to look at it."

Noah and Thomas wouldn't have any idea how hard this was for him to open up to Miriam, but she'd laid her own insecurities bare the night before, and perhaps it was only fair for him to allow her to see a little bit of his true situation, too.

Their marriage wasn't going to include sharing a home or romantic hopes, but with her father gone, he could feel that things were changing between them. Leroy's influence was fading away, and maybe they could move forward in their relationship with a little more trust and mutual respect.

Fannie and Silas wouldn't see their relationship as a success...and neither would anyone else in this community. Noah and Thomas both knew what happy marriages looked like now that they had their own. But it could be an improvement for Amos and Miriam.

Maybe *Gott* could bless them with a single step forward.

When Amos got home, he brushed down the horses and sent them out to the pasture. Then he gathered up the ledgers and headed into the house. It smelled of fragrant beef pie and home-baked bread—the aroma making his stomach rumble in response to it.

The women weren't cooking, though. *Mammi* was seated in her easy chair, which was pulled up next to a window overlooking the backyard, and Miriam sat at the kitchen table with one of his work shirts on her lap, sewing a split seam with a needle and thread. They both looked up as the screen door bounced shut behind him.

Amos paused in the doorway, and when Miriam saw him, some color went into her cheeks. She looked down at the shirt on her lap and continued sewing.

His shirt in her hands felt strangely intimate. He hadn't wanted her to be doing anything extra around here. Cooking and cleaning was fine, and obviously *Mammi* would need her help, but having her going over his clothing and mending the tears and worn spots—that felt like the work of more than a woman in the home. That felt like a wife's tender care, and he didn't want to be left with her neat, tight stitches in his clothing when she left again—a reminder of all the feminine, gentle contribution that he couldn't expect anymore.

"*Mammi* asked if I'd mend it," she said, as if she

needed to explain herself. Maybe she felt the intimacy involved with the chore, too.

From where she sat by the back window, *Mammi* shot Amos an exaggeratedly innocent look. "It needed mending, dear."

"Thank you," Amos said. "Did *Mammi* also tell you that I sew up my own seams when they split?"

"No," Miriam said, and her gaze flickered toward the old woman.

"He sews like he's hocing hard ground," *Mammi* said with a short laugh, miming the action. "He hacks at it. So *yah*, he closes a seam, but…" She shook her head.

Miriam started to laugh, and Amos was forced to join in.

"I'm not that bad," Amos said, and *Mammi* just shook her head again.

Amos put his ledgers down on the corner of the kitchen table, and then went back to the mudroom to wash his hands. When he returned, Miriam was just snipping the thread. She shook out the shirt and looked it over.

"It's in good shape now," she said, and she passed it over to him. "Dinner's ready. I just need to set the table."

Miriam paused at the ledgers, glancing down at him. He could see her piqued interest at the sight of them.

"Do you have more work to do tonight?" she asked. She reached out and touched the corner of the top ledger, and then pulled her hand back.

"I do," he said. "There's some discrepancy in my tallying, and I need to find it."

"Are you going to ask Miriam to help?" *Mammi* asked pointedly.

Amos bent down and kissed his grandmother's cheek.

"I was going to, *Mammi*," he said quietly. "I was just getting to it."

Mammi smiled at him gently. "There is no harm in needing her, dear. Helping each other is what our whole community is based on."

But it had never been what his marriage with Miriam had been based on... Their marriage had been more of a power struggle as he tried to prove to her that he was man enough to take care of her.

"Do you think you could look at the books for me, Miriam?" Amos asked, raising his voice. "*Mammi*'s right—I do need the help. I can't find this error."

"I'd be happy to," Miriam replied, and she shot him a smile. "I miss getting my hands into some financial statements. It's as satisfying as bread dough."

She always did have a way of expressing herself, and she'd never been quite like any other Amish woman.

"Thank you," he said. "I appreciate it."

All the same, his stomach knotted up. She'd find the mistake, he was sure, and it would undoubtedly be something he'd recorded improperly. So she'd be seeing his error. She'd also see exactly how successful he was—no more and no less. And when she saw how close they came to the line each month, he had a feeling that she'd look at him just a little bit differently.

Maybe this was good for his own character—letting go of his pride and desire to appear more successful than he was to earn his wife's respect. This would have to be part of their new dynamic. If she didn't respect him as the man he was, no amount of money would change it.

Maybe *Gott* was teaching him to stop trying to be something that he wasn't.

When dinner was finished, Miriam did the dishes with Amos's help. She told him he didn't need to, but he'd ignored it, and gone about cleaning off the table and bringing dishes to the sink, anyway. When they'd finished cleaning, *Mammi* dozed in her easy chair again, a breeze from an open window cooling her face, and Miriam and Amos settled down at the kitchen table with the stack of ledgers.

Miriam had been looking forward to this—she'd never had such an up-close look at her husband's business before. She'd wondered about it in the past, and her *daet* had had a few opinions about Redemption Carpentry, but Amos had never given her anything more than a cursory tour of the shop in their first year of marriage. He'd kept quiet about anything else to do with his business.

"So what's the problem?" Miriam asked.

"I'm out about five hundred dollars on paper and I can't find where I made the mistake," he said.

"Can I take a look?" She put hand on the top ledger.

"I'll show you where—" He opened it, flipped back a few pages, and she noticed his hesitation before he put it in front of her.

The lines of numbers were all neat and color-coded. She was able to easily follow the rhythm of the money coming in and out of this particular account. She worked for the better part of an hour mentally tallying up the numbers until she spotted the sudden loss of money. It was a calculation error—an expense that was written down for an order that had never been picked up, and somehow, it hadn't been included in the running tally.

"There—" she said. "I found your problem. Five hundred dollars for wood and various parts that never made it into the tally."

"Where?" Amos bent down, and his strong arm brushed hers. He smelled warm and faintly of wood. He was so tall and strong, and something inside of her longed to just lean her cheek against the solid muscle. The sudden, unbidden thought surprised her, and she felt her face heat. She reached past him, underlining the item in pencil.

"Right… I can't believe I missed it. I must have gone over that section ten times!"

Amos looked down at her, and she felt her breath catch as she tipped her chin up to meet his gaze. Those dark, intense eyes, his thick, dense beard—she dropped her gaze.

"Do you keep track of your expenses every month?" she asked, clearing her throat. This was territory she was more comfortable with.

"I have a general idea of what it costs to run the place," he said.

"So not a tailored monthly expense report?" she asked.

"No."

She nodded. "Because if I look from the beginning of last month—" She flipped back and picked up a pencil and pad of paper, jotting down numbers as she pulled a finger down the tallies of numbers. When she got to the end of the month, she nodded. "*Yah.* That's what I thought."

"What?" he asked.

"Here—" She did some quick arithmetic in her head and added it up. "This is what it cost you to run your shop last month. And this is what you made." She circled the second number. "You didn't make enough to cover your expenses."

"*Yah*, but the month before we were paid out for some big projects, and we had money left over," he replied.

"Let me take a look at the last six months—" She reached for another ledger and Amos put his hand over hers, stopping her.

"I don't need help with that," he said firmly.

"Amos, the fact that you have stayed in business all this time and have a steady flow of clients says that you are good at what you do," she said. "But even the most talented craftsman can be run under for a lack of attention to detail. My *daet*—"

"I didn't ask for your father's words of wisdom," he said curtly.

"Then what about mine?" she asked. "I can tell you what I see! Do you care about that?"

Mammi woke up from her sleep. She sucked in a breath and pulled herself up a little straighter in the chair. Miriam and Amos both looked in her direction, and Miriam couldn't help but feel like they were a couple of *kinner* getting caught for squabbling.

"Are you two spatting again?" *Mammi* asked, her voice tired.

"No, *Mammi*," Amos said quickly. "Of course not. We're just…"

"…talking business," Miriam concluded for him, and he cast her a rueful smile.

"So you are," *Mammi* said, and shook her head. "Do you think you could put a pin in that, and help me get ready for bed? I need my pills…"

"*Yah*, of course." Miriam stood up and put her pencil down next to the pad of paper, then went to *Mammi*'s side. She helped her to stand, and together they went into the sitting room where *Mammi*'s bed was. Miriam glanced back over her shoulder before they left the kitchen, and Amos stood there by the table, his hands limp at his sides. He looked deflated—was that her fault?

"At a time like this, he needs all the help he can get," *Mammi* said as Miriam helped her to sit down on the side of her bed.

Miriam went to a chest of drawers and took out a clean nightgown.

"He sees my opinions as a threat," Miriam said. "I don't think he'll take my advice."

"He sees your old *daet*'s opinions as judgment," *Mammi* replied.

"My father was a brilliant businessman," Miriam said.

Mammi caught Miriam's gaze and held it. "My dear girl, I am about to follow your father in the direction he went, so trust me when I tell you that I have infinite sympathy for your loss, and for your father's. No one is ready to die. Your father might have been a brilliant businessman, but he had a habit of treating everyone like a business deal. And people, Miriam—" *Mammi* let out a slow breath "—people are not so easy to line up. And they don't all cooperate like employees."

Miriam helped *Mammi* dress for bed, then pulled the covers back to allow her to lay down in crisp, clean sheets.

"My father was very loving," Miriam said softly. "I don't know what you heard about him—"

"To you," *Mammi* said. "He was very loving to you… Was he equally understanding for Amos?"

Miriam was silent. No, her *daet* was not. But he had a daughter to protect, and he'd wanted the very best for Miriam.

"I can't solve your issues with your husband," *Mammi* went on, "although I would dearly love to. But think about what I've said. Maybe it will help."

Miriam sat on the edge of *Mammi*'s bed and looked at *Mammi*'s pale face.

"When so many people respected him so deeply," Miriam said, "I don't understand why Amos didn't."

"Because they wanted something different from your *daet*," *Mammi* said. "They wanted his business advice to help them achieve a portion of what he had during his life, or possibly they wanted a donation to their charitable cause. It is very easy to show deference and respect when you stand to gain."

"And Amos didn't stand to gain from him?" Miriam asked with a short laugh. "He could have learned so much from my *daet*!"

"He didn't want what they wanted," *Mammi* said, and she reached out and nudged a Bible closer to Miriam. "He didn't want his business advice. He said he wanted your father's respect, but as his grandmother, I knew his heart a little better than that. What Amos wanted from your *daet* was love."

Miriam paused, staring at the old woman. "Love?"

"My son, Aaron, had problems of his own. He was very gruff, and his wife suffered from depression. He withheld his wife's medication because he didn't believe in it. Didn't Amos tell you about this?"

"A little," she admitted.

"Amos had to grow up a little faster than other children, and he never did have a kind, solid father to show him the way," she went on. "And when my husband died, he didn't have a *dawdie*, either. A boy needs a father…" *Mammi*'s voice caught. "Your husband didn't want advice or judgment from his father-in-law. He wanted love." She was silent for a moment, and then she nudged the Bible again. "Please…just open it at random and read whatever your eye falls on."

Miriam's father was a tough and crusty old man, and even his own *kinner* had to read beyond his brusque demeanor to see how he really felt about them. They had longed for some of the same affection Amos had missed out on, too. And given her father's personality, Amos might have wanted something that was too much to ask.

Miriam did as *Mammi* asked, and the Bible opened to the end of Proverbs.

"'Who can find a virtuous woman? for her price is far above rubies. The heart of her husband doth safely trust in her, so that he shall have no need of spoil. She will do him good and not evil all the days of her life…'"

The words were familiar ones—words her own *daet* had raised her on. Leroy Schwartz had shown his daughter how to run a business, how to make money grow, how to think ahead to possible pitfalls and how to throw her heart into her work. A good woman worked hard, and used her intelligence.

You have both of those attributes, Miriam, her father used to tell her. *I couldn't be more proud.*

"'Many daughters have done virtuously, but thou excellest them all. Favor is deceitful, and beauty is vain: but a woman that feareth the Lord, she shall be praised. Give her of the fruit of her hands; and let her own works praise her in the gates.'"

Miriam looked up from her reading as she came to the end of the book of Proverbs, and she found *Mammi*'s eyes still open.

"I think you were a wife like this," Miriam said.

"We all try," *Mammi* replied. "We all fall short."

Except Miriam had fallen much shorter. She'd been hardworking, smart, dedicated to the task at hand, and yet she hadn't been able to hold their relationship together. If making a man happy were simply about a woman's willingness to work hard, she would have been fine. But there had been more to it.

"I'll let you sleep," Miriam said softly.

"Good night, dear," *Mammi* replied.

Miriam tiptoed out of the room and back to the kitchen. The ledgers were all picked up again, and Amos sat at the table, a cup of water in front of him.

"Can I work out a budget for you?" Miriam asked, pausing at the table.

Amos looked up at her, pressed his lips together. "It's okay. I'll figure it out."

"Amos." She pulled out a chair and sat down. "Let me help you." She could see the old stubbornness in his jaw. "Let's leave my *daet* out of this, okay? *Mammi* explained that maybe I…push my father onto you more than I should."

"You do, a little," Amos said.

Miriam nodded. "I'm sorry. He could be difficult, and if it's worth anything, even us *kinner* had to guess at how he felt for us sometimes. It's just the way he was. But if you spent enough time with him, his love made it through, and you knew…"

Amos nodded, silent.

"The thing is, Amos, regardless of who taught me, I know how businesses thrive, and I know how they fail—"

"My business is not failing," Amos said quietly.

"No, but you are running very close to the line!" she countered. "You need to either raise your prices, or get more business. Raising your prices can be risky. You can raise them a little to match inflation—people understand that. But a better way to get more business is to advertise."

"People know about us," Amos said. "We're the best Amish-run carpentry shop in this area."

"*Yah*, a certain number of people know about you. How do you grow that?"

"I let our work speak for itself," he replied.

He was so noble, so good…and so unwilling to bend!

"That won't work," she said. "Has it so far?"

"We've been steadily growing," he replied.

"Not fast enough to make up the difference," she replied. "You have two full-time employees as well as yourself, and your expenses keep growing, because your supplies cost more every year, too. Amos, you have to look broader. You have Amish customers, but you need the Englishers."

"I've dealt with Englishers!" he snapped. "They're always pushing for a deal!"

"Then push back!" she said. "You have a business to run! And if you're going to get the word out to the Englishers, then you need to get some radio ads."

"Radio?" he frowned. "No. That's not our way."

"But it's their way," she said. "You have to put ads where you'll find your customers, and local radio is a great place to do it. Englishers listen to it while they drive, my *daet*—" She stopped herself. "Forget who told me about it. But I've seen those radio ads work wonders. A few days after they first were aired, there was a spike in new customers—all English."

Amos stood up. "I don't need more advertisement."

"Everyone needs more advertisement," she said. "Some can't afford it—"

"I can afford it just fine!" he said. "Miriam, I have run this business my way all these years, and I've done just fine."

Miriam met his gaze, and instead of that warmth she'd seen earlier, there was glittering irritation. This wasn't about her *daet* anymore, and she felt tears rise in her eyes.

"Do you know the verses I read to *Mammi* tonight?" she asked, her voice wavering.

"I heard them," he said, his voice low. "The wife of noble character from Proverbs."

"She worked hard, and she was smart," Miriam said earnestly. "She did her husband good all the days of his life. Let me do you good, Amos…"

They were silent, and Amos broke the eye contact first, looking down at his work-roughened hands.

"She also lived with her husband," Amos said quietly. "It's not the same with us."

Miriam's heart sped up, and she blinked back the tears.

"We might have a different way, you and I, but I am very much your wife, Amos Lapp!" she snapped. "Just try and marry someone else, and you'll find out how very married you are. And do you know what I think? You don't *want* a wife of noble character who can help your business thrive. You don't want a smart, talented woman at your side. You want to do it on your own and prove to me that you never did need me!"

"I have been doing it on my own!" he said. "And what is so wrong with a man wanting to be a man? I want to be the one who provides! I want to give my wife a proper life, to let her live without worry about money or debt, and I want her to trust that as her husband I have things under control!"

"Do you want me to just turn off my brain?" she asked, shaking her head.

"I want you to have a little faith in me!" he retorted.

It was difficult to have faith in a man who refused to let her see anything. It was difficult for a woman to put her entire future into the hands of a man who knew less about business than she did, and wouldn't let her see any of the details that would let her benefit him. But he was right—they weren't living together. So it was different.

Miriam nodded. "Fine. I'll back off."

Amos picked up the pile of ledgers, and his jaw

tensed. "Thank you for finding the error. I appreciate your help."

"*Yah*. No problem," she breathed.

That was all the help that he wanted—one clerical error. She had so much more to offer, and the men in her life never seemed to see it. Amos had even accepted her offer of help earlier, and he wasn't using her to her full potential.

"Would you let me look for my papers?" she asked, her throat tight.

"*Yah*." He nodded. "Of course. I've gone through this one box a few times looking for other documents, and I haven't seen yours. But you never know. I can help you—"

"No," she said with a shake of her head. "You have a restful evening. I can look alone."

Her last hope of providing for herself with any amount of dignity at this point in her life was to find those papers that proved the strip mall was hers.

Chapter Nine

When Amos went to bed that night, the kerosene lamp was still lit in the kitchen, and Miriam was standing in front of a stack of papers, sorting through them and putting them into separate piles. He hadn't asked her to organize those papers for him, but she was doing it, anyway.

He couldn't sleep yet, and he didn't want to go downstairs and argue with his wife again. She was only trying to help, and she wasn't doing any harm. Besides, she needed to find her documents.

He'd hurt her feelings tonight—he could see that much—but he wasn't sure what piece of uncomfortable truth had been the culprit.

Was she angry that he didn't want to use her idea for advertising on the radio? She made it seem so simple, but how on earth was he supposed to make that happen? He didn't have any of the technology that Englishers used for such things. Did they just…talk into their phones? Did they have computer programs that did it? That wasn't an option for an Amish man! They had small businesses and small farms, and by not getting too big, they stayed closer to their communities, and closer to home. He'd never questioned that before. There was no shame in staying small!

But now, Miriam was suggesting growth using Englisher media that he wasn't comfortable with, and sitting in his bedroom just over the kitchen, he wasn't going to sleep. So he got up and he sat in a little chair next to the window with his Bible on his lap.

She might not like a husband who was the traditional man, who cared for his wife and didn't expose her to worry. She might not like that he wouldn't give up control in his own company, and he might irritate her something fierce just by existing.

But that was okay. He was still the man of this house and would sit up until he heard her go to bed. Then he'd go to sleep. Call him old-fashioned, or call him too stubborn, but he felt in his bones that protecting the women in his home was still his responsibility.

He opened his Bible, and an underlined passage stood out at him. It was in First Peter: *Likewise, ye husbands, dwell with them according to knowledge, giving honor unto the wife, as unto the weaker vessel, and as being heirs together of the grace of life; that your prayers be not hindered.*

This was a verse that he'd read over and over again during that first year of marriage, and in the years since she left. These had been accusing words—ones that drove him to his knees, asking *Gott* to change him, and forgive him, and show him how to do better. In fact, he'd read this passage and prayed the same prayer only a few weeks before Miriam arrived.

He could see the meaning in the verse very clearly—if he wasn't honoring his wife, and if he wasn't treating her as an equal, then *Gott* wasn't going to be listening to his prayers. There was no righteous confidence for a man who didn't have peace in his own home.

Lord, he prayed. *I don't want to be a difficult husband, but she isn't an easy woman to understand. Show me how to do this...*

He put his Bible aside and went back to his closet. He pulled down the partially carved trinket box, and he ran his fingers over it. He still felt a surge of guilt at never having finished it. He carried it over to where his lamp sat on the windowsill, and he pulled out a knife.

It had been nearly ten years since he'd worked on this box, but he could remember the exact pattern he'd been working on, and he could see the finished product in his mind's eye. He started to carve, the sharp knife biting into the wood. He didn't know how to honor his wife. He was better than his *daet* had been to his *mamm*, but it wasn't nearly good enough. Maybe finishing this gift at long last could be a start.

An hour later, Miriam's footsteps went up the stairs and into her bedroom. Her door shut with a soft click.

He continued carving, his hands sure as he worked out the vines and thorns of the rosebush twining around the outer edge. He wanted to be right with *Gott*, and he knew he wouldn't be, unless he was also right with his wife.

The next day at work went smoothly enough, but Amos's mind was on those numbers that Miriam had pointed out. If he had to be completely honest with himself, he'd be more comfortable if he had a little more wiggle room in his budget. If he could sell some smaller items every day, the sorts of things that cost less to make and could bring in a bigger profit, that would be incredibly helpful. With more Englisher customers buying things like spice racks, ornamental mailboxes, quilt racks and jewelry boxes, he could have more money left over for emergencies, or for putting toward retirement. A man might not want to retire, but his body might insist upon it.

If he asked *Mammi*'s opinion, he knew what it would be—listen to his wife. But *Mammi*'s priorities weren't completely locked on his business success. She wanted to bring him and Miriam back together under the same roof. What she didn't realize was that having Miriam here, having her help, her cooking, her mending his shirts…it wasn't making things easier on a heart level. Because he had never asked his wife to leave—she'd left on her own, and he didn't think that she'd willingly come back just because of a couple of weeks of getting along.

After they'd closed up the carpentry shop for the day and Thomas and Noah headed home to their own wives and *kinner*, Amos hitched up his buggy and set out for home. When he arrived, he took care of the horses, and then he came up the steps, past some laundry hanging on the line, and into the mudroom.

He glanced into the kitchen and *Mammi*'s chair was empty. His heart gave a little jump.

"Where is she?" he asked.

"Sleeping," Miriam said. "And hello."

"Sorry," he said. "Hi. Let me just wash my hands and get my boots off."

Miriam came to the mudroom door and leaned a shoulder against the frame as he soaped up his hands.

"The doctor came by today," she said.

"What did he say?" Amos asked.

"He said that she'll be sleeping more often now," Miriam said. "And if she needs more pain medication, we should give her whatever she needs to be comfortable."

Amos nodded, dried his hands and exchanged a sad look with Miriam.

"I'm glad you're here with her," he said. "I'm going to take tomorrow off to spend some time with her, I think. If she's sleeping more, I hate to lose time with her."

"I think she'd appreciate it," Miriam said with a nod, her eyes misting. "Come in and have dinner. I made chicken pie with some salad on the side. If you're still hungry, I also made some apple crisp."

It sounded delicious, and he nodded his thanks and followed her into the kitchen.

"Did *Mammi* eat?" he asked.

"She had a little apple crisp," Miriam said with a smile.

That was good to hear. He peeked into the bedroom to see *Mammi* sleeping peacefully, her thin, weathered hand resting on her Bible. Then he went back to the table.

Miriam dished up two plates of food, and then sat down with him. She looked at him expectantly, and he bowed his head. This was his home, and it was his place to ask the blessing.

"For this food we are about to eat," he prayed, "make us truly thankful."

The problem was, he *was* thankful for the food, for the woman who'd cooked it, even for the heartache that she brought back up for him. He was thankful for all of this—the time with his grandmother, and for the faith that he clung to in these difficult times. It was letting go of it all that was going to hurt the most.

He raised his head and plunged his fork into the flaky crust, chicken gravy pooling over his plate. He nodded as Miriam offered him some salad on the side. He'd worked hard, and he hadn't eaten any lunch today, his mind being on other things, so he was hungry now.

"I wanted to ask you," Amos said. "If I were to...do a radio ad...how would I do it?"

He kept his eyes on his plate and took another bite. He wasn't sure how she'd react—condescension, a story about her *daet*'s superior business skills...

"Are you really thinking of doing it?" she asked.

He glanced up, and to his surprise, he saw genuine happiness in her face.

"It's a good idea," he admitted. "And if I could make a little extra, it would make saving for retirement a little easier."

She smiled at that. "*Yah*. That's the thing. You do a lot of large items that have high overhead cost to build, meaning that you're putting a lot of time and energy into pieces that aren't going to make you as much profit. Smaller pieces that use less material and time could make up the difference, and Englisher tourists as well as Englishers living in the area are your perfect customers for this."

"Hmm." He chewed, listening to her talk. She had more ideas—not just the radio ad. She thought he should put up ads for his shop at the bus depot where the tourists arrived, showing pictures of the smaller items, touting them as genuine Amish.

"That sounds silly," he said. "I suppose anything I touch is genuine Amish."

"Isn't that great?" she said. "It's all about getting word out, and there are plenty of people who would love nothing more than to buy Amish-made merchandise. Honestly, Amos, what I wouldn't do for this kind of foot traffic in Edson!"

Her happy smile faded, and she put down her fork. For a moment, she sat in silence.

"What?" he said.

"Oh, it's nothing." Miriam rose to her feet and picked up her plate. He watched her go to the counter and deposit her plate there.

"Miriam," he said, and she turned toward him.

"It's just an emotional time," she said. "I'm fine."

But she wasn't. He could see that plain as day. She'd been happy talking about marketing his business up until she'd mentioned going home. Did she not want to leave?

"I found my papers," she said. "They were down the side of the box, under a flap."

"Oh, good…" He felt his earlier optimism start to fade, too. "I'm glad you found them."

"I'll have my own strip mall to run," she said. "It's a start. And I am serious about opening a new business, too."

"With your marketing sense, you'll be jumping ahead in no time," he said.

"*Yah*, it's…ideal." But her voice caught, and his heart tugged toward her in response.

Amos rose to his feet, the food forgotten. He crossed the kitchen and caught her hand. She looked up at him, her eyelashes wet, and without thinking better of it, he pulled her into his arms and against his chest.

It was a long-buried instinct with her—pulling her close—and she fit in his arms in just the same way she used to. He was afraid to look down at her, but he tightened his arms around her, and rested his cheek against her hair and *kapp*.

"Miriam," he murmured, and when she looked up, he followed another long-buried instinct, and he bent down, covering her lips with his.

They'd always had such passionate kisses after arguments, and there had been something about the relief of falling into each other's arms all over again that felt the same.

Except they hadn't been fighting this time.

They'd been getting along…

Amos had a way of looking at her just before he kissed her that made her stomach tumble…and ten years hadn't changed that a bit. Feeling his restrained strength in his gentle touch, her heart skipped a beat.

Miriam felt the warmth of Amos's strong arms as he pulled her closer against him, and up onto her tiptoes. His beard tickled her face, and she felt all the frustration and tension inside of her melt away. There always had been something about Amos's kisses that had scrambled her mind and left her a little weak in the knees, and feeling his arms around her again felt more familiar than she had a right to. It had been a good many years since they'd shared a kiss, but it was like no time had passed at all, and they'd simply fallen back together.

His touch, his breath, the feeling of his lips against hers… It was like the time between that tumultuous first year and today had collapsed together like a folding fan.

Standing here in the kitchen with his arms around her, the heat from cooking still hanging in the air and that same old feeling of wild relief coursing through her, she didn't want to move. It was a relief to be in his arms again, to feel his touch, his breath on her face, to smell that musky scent of sunshine and woodworking. She didn't want to think, or move, or disturb the moment so that it would flutter away.

Amos pulled back, and she blinked her eyes open. For a moment, neither of them said anything, and Miriam held her breath. Then when Amos leaned toward her again, she felt a surge of misgiving. There were so many reasons not to kiss her husband, and she shook her head, and pulled out of his arms.

"We can't do this, Amos," she said. Her voice sounded too loud.

"We're married," he replied with a rueful smile. "Of all the people who have the right to kiss each other, I think we do."

That wasn't what she was talking about, and he knew it.

"We've done this before," she said, softening her tone. "We fight, we argue, we make up, and we do it again. I can't do this anymore!"

"Except we weren't fighting," he murmured. "Not this time."

"Only because we're trying our best to make this a peaceful time for *Mammi*," she said. "If it weren't for her, we would be."

Amos licked his lips, then took a step back. "Maybe I shouldn't have kissed you, but I do care about whatever it was that made you look so heartbroken a minute ago."

"I'm not heartbroken…" She swallowed, and as if to prove her wrong, tears misted her eyes.

"You are…"

She looked around the kitchen, at the newly familiar table and chairs, the cupboards that used to be hers, the chipped blue teapot that sat on the counter, still warm with leftover tea.

"I'm going back to Edson to run my own business," she said softly, and she looked up at Amos, then wiped an errant tear from her cheek. "That's all."

And she'd be forced to walk away from this house all over again—put it behind her, and go start over in Edson, where people knew and respected her, and where there was no husband to cook for, no old woman to care for… No one who needed her.

"You wanted that life in Edson," he said. "Don't you?"

"I still want it," she said. "But I suppose coming back has reminded me of all the things I'd wanted when we first got married—all those silly, girlish hopes I had for our life together."

"I had a few hopes, too," he said quietly.

"Oh?" Was this where he told her where she'd let him down?

"I'm just saying that when you leave, it's going to be hard for me, too," he said. "But I won't apologize for kissing my own wife. There was no sin in that."

Kissing him had always been easier than talking to him. It had been easier than facing their differences, or finding solutions. Of course, a married couple should have a life filled with affection and love, but they hadn't used married love to tie them together—they'd used it to forget their last fight.

"Amos, I can't do this," she whispered. "I'm tired and I'm sad. I'm dealing with my father's death, and your grandmother's illness, and—" She swallowed. "I'm not at my strongest."

Because when she was at her strongest, she could see her way through all of this. She could see the other end—when she got past the heartbreak again, and she realized that while neither of them had dreamed of this separate life, they were happier apart.

"I know. Me, neither," he said. "But having you here is nice all the same."

For now. But for how long? Their relationship didn't have what it took to last, and it was easy to forget that in emotional moments like this one.

"Natasha Zook was telling me why she was willing to become Amish," Miriam said. "Because if you get to know that woman, her becoming Amish makes no sense! She's not even Mennonite! She's English to the core, and yet here she is dressed in Amish clothing, burning her food on a woodstove and driving around in a pickup truck." Miriam shook her head. "And she's determined to be Amish. Why?"

"The Amish faith is pure and she can see the Christian love we have here—"

"The Amish faith is many wonderful things," Miriam said, cutting him off. "But that's not why. Her decision was far from theological, Amos. She said she was willing to do it because she loved him. But more than love, she said she truly believed that *Gott* had created her and Wollie for each other. She says no other man can make her happier than Wollie can, and she's willing to uproot her entire life, alienate her family, who thinks she crazy for doing this, and start this brand-new life that she knows very little about."

"For him," Amos said, his voice low.

"For him." She nodded. "Did you ever think that *Gott* looked down on this planet some thirty-five years ago and decided to create the perfect woman for you in the form of…me?"

Amos blinked at her, and she felt the heat in her face.

"Have you ever considered that?" she pressed. "You and I decided that we wanted to get married— we wanted to *be* married. It wasn't about us being such a perfect match. It was about us both being left over!"

"Maybe *Gott* was working with that," Amos said.

"Then you must also think that *Gott* isn't a very good matchmaker," Miriam said. "Because you and I are terribly matched. We were just too foolish to see it, and we didn't ask for anyone else's opinion before we insisted that we were ready to marry. We thought we could make our marriage something beautiful with sheer willpower."

Amos was silent.

"We are married, Amos," she said. "But we aren't

like Wollie and Natasha. We aren't like Fannie and Silas. I married you, but I wasn't willing to have *kinner* with you. I wasn't willing to risk my health to grow our family."

"I understand that now," he said.

"Yah," she said. "But I also realized that my logical approach to all of these things tells me a lot, too. There was a lot I *wasn't* willing to do for our relationship. And I think what you are willing to do is just as telling as what you aren't."

Because she hadn't been willing to take any leaps of faith with Amos. And when she'd heard Natasha talk about her love for her husband, Miriam had felt something she hadn't felt in a long time—envy.

It was easy to be around people who'd married for logical reasons and were kind and decent to each other. She didn't feel so different from them—she'd married for similar reasons, even if it hadn't worked out as positively. And then she heard the story of a woman who'd married a man from a completely different culture because she'd fallen in love with him. And she'd poured herself into his culture because she believed that *Gott* had created them from embryos to be together.

Some people might mock that kind of romantic view, but Miriam couldn't bring herself to. She couldn't make fun of it, because she did believe in a *Gott* who cared about the details. She did believe that *Gott* guided their steps and showered blessings upon them. But somehow, Miriam had missed *Gott*'s guidance with the most important decision of her life.

"I don't know what to say," Amos said at last.

"It's okay," she said. "We weren't in love with each other, Amos. And we thought it wouldn't matter."

Amos stayed silent, and she felt tears rising inside of her. She wouldn't cry over this—not in front of him.

"I'm going to check the horses," she said, standing up.

It wasn't her job, but keeping busy was easier than focusing on the happiness she may very well have given up because she was in too much of a hurry and had wanted to make things happen on her own.

Miriam headed for the door.

She didn't need her husband's kisses, or his sympathy. She needed to get her balance back.

Chapter Ten

Amos drove to the shop the next morning to tell Noah and Thomas that he wouldn't be working that day, and as he drove his horses down the familiar roads, his mind was stuck on the kiss from the night before. He wasn't sorry, and he wouldn't apologize for it. They'd doomed each other to a life without romance, and if all he had to think about at night was a single, honest kiss that they'd shared, then he'd hold on to it.

And yet, he knew that brief moment of weakness would come with its own punishment. The most honest moments of his life always did. Like when, as a ten-year-old, he'd finally demanded that his father pay for his mother's medication after she had taken to bed in depression. He'd told his father that she would have her pills, or Amos would start telling anyone who would listen what was happening behind those walls. Let the bishop and the elders come—Amos would tell them an earful! And his father had believed him. He pulled out his wallet and handed the cash over. But his relationship with his father had never been the same. His *daet* had never been the same, either... He was more cowed. More wary. He stopped thundering and booming when he was angry, too.

When *Daet* died the next winter during a bad bout of the flu, Amos had felt like he was partly to blame. He knew that he'd broken his father's spirit, and while he'd meant it for good, there were a whole tangle of consequences.

His *mamm* had never felt quite right about taking the pills again, either. If Amos had reined in his emotions and dealt with it differently, would his mother have taken her medication without guilt?

Amos arrived later than usual, and Noah was just flipping the sign in the front window to Open.

"I'm not staying today," Amos said. "*Mammi* is getting weaker. I wanted to take a day with her while I can."

"*Yah*, understandable," Noah said. "Is she in much pain?"

Thomas came out of the woodshop and leaned against the door frame.

"The medication helps with the pain," Amos said. "But it also makes her sleep a lot, and...maybe that's a blessing, but—"

Thomas came into the showroom, and they all stood in silence for a moment.

"It's good that you'll have time with her," Thomas said. "How are things with Miriam there?"

"Miriam is great," Amos said. "She's helpful, she's efficient, *Mammi* just loves having her back in the house and..." He sighed. "I'm not saying that it isn't complicated. You're both married men now, so I'm sure you understand. Miriam is my wife—she's not just a woman in the home. She's...*my wife*."

Did they understand all the emotion that was locked in those two little words, *my wife*? Because he'd taken vows before *Gott* and his community that he'd love and care for her. She might not have wanted either of those things in the end, but it didn't stop that he'd vowed to do it. There was something about a wedding—a woman in her wedding apron, a bishop to give the blessing— that locked things down inside of a man whether it was good for him in the long run or not.

"Do you think she might stay, after all?" Noah asked quietly.

Amos shook his head. "No. I don't. We both know how this is going to end. It just isn't easy. That's all."

And it was his burden to bear.

Thomas shuffled his feet uncomfortably, and Noah and Amos looked over at him.

"Patience and I have a meeting with an adoption agent today," Thomas said. "I know this is bad timing with *Mammi* being so sick, but we still long for *kinner*, and this is a chance at growing our family. If I could leave a bit early that would be really helpful. I can come back later on and get more work done in the shop if we're behind—"

"Don't worry about it," Amos replied. "A meeting with an adoption agent is really big. Is there any news? A baby, perhaps?"

"This is a long process," Thomas said. "They told us to expect it to take a while, so we aren't getting our hopes up just yet. I don't want Patience to get disappointed again—" Thomas glanced toward his brother, and Noah froze.

That was a complicated history between the brothers. The first child that Patience had thought she would adopt had been Eve's, and Noah had married Eve and was raising her child as his own. Patience still didn't have another baby in her arms...

"I don't mean it like that," Thomas said. "Samuel is your son now, Noah, and there are no hard feelings there. But when we thought that we were going to adopt Samuel, Patience had her heart in it completely. And if this little boy ends up going to another home, I just don't want her heartbroken again."

"So there is a child?" Noah asked.

"There is a little boy who needs a home. He's two years old, and he's been in the foster system for a while. He has food allergies, and he has some attachment issues because he's been to a few different foster homes already—" Thomas sucked in a breath. "He'd need stability and love—that's what the agent said—and we have that in great supply. He's been through so much upheaval in his young life already that he just needs a home that won't change on him again."

"I'll be praying for you," Noah said earnestly. "Eve and I both will."

"Thank you," Thomas replied. "Patience and I have been praying for the child *Gott* has for us, and I just feel—" Thomas shrugged. "I feel like *Gott* is working in this. But only *Gott* knows what He has in store for us."

"*Mammi* would say that *Gott* is working in every little detail," Noah said.

The men all smiled sadly at the mention of *Mammi* and for a moment they fell silent. Amos looked at the young men he'd raised in his home with *Mammi*'s help, and he saw the emotion brimming in their eyes. They loved her, too.

"She's a woman of faith," Amos said. "She's been praying all this time for both of you—I'm sure she'll be glad to pray for this, too. When you need to leave, you can just put up a sign saying that we're closing early today, and we'll see people in the morning. Family first." Amos patted Thomas on the shoulder. "Always."

"Thanks," Thomas said with a nod and a grateful smile.

"I'd better head back," Amos said. *Mammi* was waiting.

On the way, Amos prayed silently for Thomas and Patience. They'd been through a lot already. When Eve Schrock came to Redemption to give birth to her child and give it up for adoption, they'd thought they were getting an answer to their prayer to adopt a baby. But when Noah and Eve fell in love, Thomas and Patience had tearfully handed the infant back to his mother and stepped back to allow Noah and Eve to raise her son. That had been heartbreaking for Thomas and Patience, but they'd put family first—that was the Amish way. That was *Gott*'s way.

And now, they had another chance to grow their family, and Amos prayed earnestly that *Gott* would grant the deepest desires of their hearts and give them this little boy into their care, if it be *Gott*'s will.

It was always hardest to add that last little bit to a prayer: *If it be Your will, Lord.*

There were other prayers deep in Amos's heart that he was afraid to even bring out into the light. Like this growing hope that Miriam might decide to stay, after all. He wouldn't say it aloud. He'd never tell Noah or Thomas…or even *Mammi* for that matter. Sometimes a man's hopes were so fragile that he didn't dare let anyone else see them.

But having Miriam here had shown him what it could be like if they lived together…what it could be like if she were truly his wife again, in his heart and in his arms. And that kiss last night had settled deep into his heart. Was it stupid of him to hang on to it like that? Probably, but he couldn't help it, either.

When Amos turned into the drive, he saw Miriam arranging a wicker chair underneath a cherry tree, an old, faded quilt spread over the grass nearby. She didn't turn right away, her attention on the job in front of her, and when he reined in the horses, he watched her work for a moment.

There was something about her presence at the house again that softened him. When she turned he hopped down from the buggy and circled around to unhitch the horses, and Miriam looked up and met his gaze. She didn't smile, or wave, but the eye contact made him catch his breath.

"What are you doing?" he called.

"*Mammi* wanted to come out and enjoy the beautiful weather," Miriam said, angling her steps in his direction. "So I'm making it comfortable for her."

The sun was already warm enough that the dew had burned off. A butterfly flitted over the tiny, growing plants in the garden, and Amos pulled off his hat and wiped his brow. It would be the kind of spring day that gave them a taste of summer.

Miriam put her hands on her hips, looking up at him as he got down from the buggy.

"Did you know that your grandfather used to take your *mammi* out on picnics every summer, just the two of them?" Miriam asked.

"Uh—" He stopped, eyed her for a moment. "I seem to remember that…"

Mammi had been telling stories that morning, it seemed.

"She said he proposed marriage on a picnic by the creek," Miriam said, and her expression was thoughtful. "On the Service Sunday their intentions were announced, she made him a picnic, and they ate it in the backyard on an old blanket. She said it was the most delicious meal she ever made."

"She has good memories," Amos said.

"I'm almost envious," Miriam said.

He smiled faintly. "I don't think my proposal to you was as good as my *dawdie*'s. I asked you to marry me on a Service Sunday, on bench at the back of the barn after everyone had left to go eat."

Miriam had been visiting some friends—an older couple, who had since passed away. It was a veiled attempt to meet a single man, truthfully. He'd known it.

Miriam's cheeks pinked. *"Yah."*

"I could have done better," he said.

"You were very serious. I still remember what you said," she replied.

"I don't," he admitted. "I was so nervous I blurted out something…that you agreed to."

"You said we were very much alike, both of us strong and deeply committed to the faith," Miriam said quietly. "And you thought we could be very happy together if we decided to be, and you wanted to know if I would be willing to marry you."

Amos looked over at her, feeling foolish at the memory. It hadn't been terribly romantic, but then, they'd hardly known each other, either. He'd been envisioning a life that never materialized—one where they had babies and raised them to be well-behaved boys and girls. He imagined dinners as a family, worship time before the *kinner* were sent up to bed…

"I'm truly sorry," he said.

"For what?" Miriam asked.

"I was obviously wrong about us being happy together if we wanted to be," he said.

Because he had wanted it…so badly.

"Oh, Amos." Miriam put a gentle hand on his arm. "We were both wrong. And we both tried. But I still have the memory of a very sweet proposal and a lovely October wedding. No one can take that from me."

But what was it worth, when they couldn't manage to live under the same roof? *Mammi* had her memories of *Dawdie*'s proposal, of their little farm wedding and of the babies they'd had who hadn't survived and the one and only son who had, and even through that heartbreak, they'd weathered it side by side. She had memories of growing old with her husband… And then *Mammi* had the bitterly sad memory of burying him in the same graveyard as the babies who had passed away

so early. They'd had a true and complete life together—
the good and the bad. What could Amos and Miriam
say? Their lives had been lived separately.

Amos looked toward the house.

"*Mammi* is waiting for you," Miriam said.

"I'll take care of the horses and then go get her,"
he said.

"Sure. I have a few things to finish out here," Miriam said.

She turned and headed back toward the picnic area
she'd been putting together, and Amos watched her go.
Then he tore his gaze away from his wife, and started
to unhitch the horses. Whatever was happening inside
of a man's heart, whatever pain he was trying to tamp
down, work didn't stop.

When Amos was finished, he headed up the steps
and into the kitchen. *Mammi* sat in her comfortable
chair and her whole face lit up when she spotted him.

"How are you feeling, *Mammi*?" he asked.

"Much better!" she said. "I can't quite stand up, but
I do feel better than I have in weeks."

"*Yah?*" He shot her a smile. "I'm glad."

"We're having a picnic—" *Mammi* motioned weakly
toward the window. "But I need help getting out there.
I've been longing for some sunlight, and some fresh air."

"Shall I carry you out?" he asked.

"Yes, please." Her smile was sweet, and she leaned
forward in her chair.

Amos bent down and scooped his hands under her
frail legs and lifted her up in his arms. She hardly
weighed anything these days, and her dress was so
loose.

"Thank you, Amos," *Mammi* said, patting his shoulder gently as he carried her out the side door and into the warm spring air. "There's nothing quite like a spring day to make you feel closer to Heaven, is there?"

Amos carefully made his way down the stairs, and Miriam hurried over to angle the chair for him so that he could place *Mammi* down in her spot in the shade under the cherry tree. He settled her in the wicker chair, and Miriam brought a pillow to put behind her back. *Mammi* looked around herself with a smile on her face.

"Would you like some strawberries, *Mammi*?" Miriam asked. "The neighbors got them from the supermarket, and I whipped up fresh cream to go with them."

"No, but thank you, dear," *Mammi* said. "I'm just not hungry. But, Amos—"

Amos bent down toward her.

"Sit down," *Mammi* said. "Let's enjoy some warm weather together."

Amos sank down to the quilt on the ground and he stretched his legs out, resting on his elbow. From where he lay, he could see the beginning of cherries on the tree above their heads, little green fruit. By the fence, he spotted a rabbit nibbling on the lush grass.

"The strangest bits of Scripture come back to you when you're at this stage of life," *Mammi* said softly.

"Oh?" Amos asked. "What verse are you thinking of?"

"'I am come into my garden, my sister, my spouse,'" *Mammi* said, her voice quiet. "'I have gathered my myrrh with my spice; I have eaten my honeycomb with my honey; I have drunk my wine with my milk: eat, O

friends; drink, yea, drink abundantly, O beloved…'"
Mammi's voice trailed away.

"Song of Songs," Amos murmured.

Mammi smiled. "I miss your *dawdie*, Amos. We had a good life together. A good, good life…"

For *Mammi*, it seemed like her days of marriage and motherhood, of love and living deeply, were only a breath away. When Amos was *Mammi*'s age, when he was looking back on his life, would he be feeling resplendent with satisfied memories like *Mammi* was? Or would he have regrets?

Miriam stood back a few paces, watching Amos and his grandmother talking quietly in the shade of the cherry tree. *Mammi* looked even smaller today, but she was brighter, somehow, happier. Maybe it was the sunshine, or having her grandson home with her during the day like it was a holiday just for her.

Looking at Amos lying on the blanket, she could remember what he looked like eleven years ago when he'd proposed so earnestly. He was still tall and handsome, although now he had the thick, bushy beard of a married man. His chest was still broad, and his arms roped with muscle from the physical labor he did every day.

She really had thought that a man as good as Amos couldn't help but be a good husband…or maybe the fault had been hers. She'd refused to have *kinner* after her sister's death. She'd always thought that after she married, she'd be able to settle into raising her *kinner* and keeping house. It was a huge amount of work to occupy a woman's time, but without the *kinner* in her future, somehow her hopes for running a business, the competition of coming out on top, came creeping back in. Maybe they would have, anyway.

Which was wrong. She wasn't even arguing that. An Amish woman wasn't supposed to compete. She was supposed to be content in the role of wife and *mamm*. But Miriam hadn't been able to.

"Where did Miriam go?" *Mammi*'s voice came to her on the breeze.

"I'm here, *Mammi*," Miriam said, and she came over to where they sat. "Can I get you anything?"

"Sit, sit," *Mammi* said, gesturing to the blanket. "I was about to tell a story."

Mammi's mind seemed to be on her late husband these days. Miriam had never met *Dawdie*. But she'd heard stories here and there about him. He had saved his brother from being crushed by a load of hay bales when he was a teenager, single-handedly lifting four- teen bales off his brother, and pulling him to safety. She'd also heard a few funny stories about *Dawdie* get- ting confused in Englisher shops, or *Dawdie* coming back with a funny quip when his brothers used to needle him. Miriam settled down on the blanket next to Amos, who shifted his legs to make room for her.

"I remember when Amos was just a little boy," *Mammi* said. "He was about as tall as the tie on my apron, and he was a rascal…"

Miriam looked over at Amos and chuckled.

"Wait—this is a story about me?" Amos said. "I thought we were going to hear about *Dawdie*!"

"So did I," Miriam said. "But this might be just as good."

"Oh, hush," *Mammi* said, a smile twinkling in her

eyes. "Amos was an only child. His mother had some difficulties in his delivery, and she wasn't able to have any more, and we had neighbors with children his age, so he'd come to visit and play. Anyway, one day, Amos was visiting us, getting a chance to play with other kids, when we had an Englisher traveling salesman stop by. They were much more common back then. This one was selling encyclopedia sets. And when he knocked on the door, he looked so bedraggled and tired that I invited him in for tea and pie. While he was eating, a storm opened up outside, so he had to stay a little longer."

Amos frowned. "I don't remember this…"

"No?" *Mammi* said. "Well, you weren't very old. Anyway, I knew I wasn't buying any encyclopedias from that man, but the man didn't know it, and he kept trying to make his sales pitch. But I didn't want to send him out into the storm, either. So I let him talk."

"I think I do remember this," Amos said. "I remember the kitchen being dark and rain coming down in a torrent and a man in an overcoat sitting at the kitchen table…"

"*Yah*, that would be the one," *Mammi* said. "Little Amos didn't like this Englisher stranger pushing me to buy something, and he seemed to think that I needed help. So he stood up just as tall as he could stand, and he said, 'My *dawdie* is working in the field, and my *daet* isn't here, so that makes me the man of this house. You leave my *mammi* alone, or I'll have to ask you to leave!'"

Miriam looked over at Amos, while *Mammi* was laughing softly to herself. Amos's cheeks grew pink, and he pulled off his hat and rubbed a hand through his hair.

"I thought I was bigger than I was," Amos said. "I remember being older than that."

"Oh, no," *Mammi* said. "You were all of five or six."

"So your nobility started young," Miriam said.

"Apparently." Amos rolled his eyes. "If you could call insulting a grown man nobility."

"I'm going to tell you something," *Mammi* said, sobering. "And I know I've told you a little bit about my son, Aaron, but there's more."

"Mammi—" Amos started.

"She needs to hear this," *Mammi* said. She looked a little paler now, and she sucked in an uneven breath.

"No, I don't think she does," Amos replied. "*Mammi*, please trust me on this—"

"Amos, you'll have to trust *me*, this time," *Mammi* replied. "She'll only understand you better if she understands your *daet*. Now, I don't have much strength, and perhaps you'll insist upon me keeping quiet… You are the man of this home…"

Amos rose to his feet now, and he looked from *Mammi*, then down at Miriam. She could see the battle on his features, and *Mammi* was right—Amos could insist upon this secret being keep, as the man of the home.

"I wouldn't give you any orders, *Mammi*," Amos said, his voice tight. "You know me better than that."

Miriam caught her breath and looked back at the old woman. She was watching her grandson with a somber look on her face, and then she continued, her voice quiet.

"My son, Aaron, wasn't a good husband," *Mammi* went on. "He didn't provide well. He used to gamble and drink, and the money he made was often spent by the time he got home on the evening of payday. I sometimes blamed the fact that I couldn't give him siblings for how he turned out. He never did have to share…" She shook her head. "But Amos was an only child, too, and he turned out to be such a wonderful young man that I suppose I'm forced to admit that it wasn't me. It was drink. It was addiction…" She sighed. "So Amos felt the immense pressure very early. Amos didn't have anyone to share with, either, but there was much less to live on. He and his mother had to find ways to hide money from Aaron to keep him from gambling it away."

"But you were so little," Miriam said softly.

Amos didn't answer. He pressed his lips together and stood braced as if for a blow.

"He didn't think he was little," *Mammi* said. "And he certainly didn't stay little. He was big for his age at ten. Aaron's drinking and gambling got worse as he got older, not better. We tried everything to get through to Aaron that he was ruining not only his life, but his wife's and son's, too. We even talked about having him shunned, but his wife did her best to keep on raising Amos on the little bit of money she could scrounge up from odd jobs and charity then hide from Aaron. And we kept bringing over groceries and doing our best to help out."

"One day, when I was about ten," Amos said, his deep voice taking up the story, "my *daet* got home from gambling, and he owed a great deal of money. They'd roughed him up, and he was looking for the deed to our acreage so that he could sell it, I think. I'd already started confronting my father about things in our home, and I wrestled that deed out of his hands—it wasn't hard. He was drunk, and I—" Amos swallowed. "I hit my father in the face with a water pitcher, knocking him out cold."

Miriam sucked in a breath and stared at him in shock. Amos—sweet, gentle Amos, hitting his own father?

"And my mother took over the family finances that day," Amos said. "I worked odd jobs, and my *mamm* and I pooled what we could make in a bank account together. She took over paying the bills, and I even put a little bit of savings aside for emergencies. My mother and I learned together, and we kept our home. My father was never allowed access to that bank account."

"*This* acreage?" Miriam asked, looking around at the familiar garden, the house, the trees.

"*Yah*, this one," Amos said. "My parents both passed away. My *daet* got a bad flu the very next year and my *mamm* had a stroke a few years after when I was about fourteen. She went into the hospital and didn't recover."

"You took good care of your *mamm*," *Mammi* said quietly. "You're a better man than your father was, and I'm proud of you. So proud."

Amos met his grandmother's tender gaze, and she saw tears mist his eyes.

"Miriam," *Mammi* said. "There are always reasons why people react the ways that they do. And your husband is no different in that. We tried to make our family look a little better for your benefit. We were embarrassed. We didn't want people to know our problems…"

"I understand," Miriam said softly. "It's okay."

"Maybe we should have told you all of this sooner," *Mammi* said. "But all the same, when I die, I won't be harboring secrets. I don't think the Lord can bless that."

They were all silent for a few beats; the birds overhead were the only noise that interrupted the stillness between them.

Amos sighed. "I think that's enough stories for now. I'm going to go check on the horses."

And he bent down, giving his grandmother a kiss on her cheek before he strode away toward the stables. Miriam watched him go, her heart hovering in her chest. The horses were fine—he was running away.

"That's why he longed for my *daet* to love him," Miriam said, tears rising in her eyes.

"Yah," Mammi said softly. "That's why."

Because his own *daet* hadn't loved him properly, and he'd been hoping that her *daet* might fill some of that emptiness. There were good reasons why Amos was the way he was, and none of those reasons were because he wasn't man enough or strong enough, or smart enough.

At last, she understood him, and that was a gift in itself. *Mammi* was right that secrets only made things harder, but it didn't change who they both were, and what they both needed.

Amos needed a dutiful wife at home who would trust him. Her trust was the key to his heart. And Miriam needed some freedom, some adventure, to have a voice in growing their business to its full potential.

Their needs didn't change, especially not Amos's. He'd needed a very different kind of woman, and the fact that he'd married her, the very opposite of what would fulfill what his aching heart needed most, made their marriage all the more tragic.

Chapter Eleven

"Are you upset with me, Aaron?" *Mammi* asked.

"It's Amos, *Mammi*," he said softly.

"Oh…yes…"

She was propped up in her bed, her eyes half-shut, but she struggled to open them all the way to look at Amos as he sat down on the edge of her bed. The room was warm, but *Mammi* had wanted an extra blanket over her legs. An open window let in some fresh air, the sound of birds twittering coming in with the early-evening sunlight. On the bed next to *Mammi* was a bowl of the strawberries from the supermarket with some whipped cream, but she refused them.

"Are you upset with me for telling Miriam what I did?" *Mammi* asked.

"No, *Mammi*," Amos said softly. "Of course not."

"You can say if you are," she whispered. "I can take it."

No, she couldn't take it, but even so, he wasn't angry with her. How could he be? His grandmother had been one of his biggest supporters growing up, and on the day he and his mother had opened that bank account, his grandmother had given him a hug and told him that he was a good boy. She'd been the difference between despondence and hope. She'd been a ray of sunlight. His throat tightened with emotion.

Mammi had tired herself out today. He could see all the signs. She'd been weaker than ever before, and she was in bed long before sunset. Noah and his family had come to see *Mammi*, and they'd all prayed together for Thomas's hopes of adoption. *Mammi* had prayed so eloquently for all of them, mentioning them each by name. She had been bright and cheerful, but all her energy seemed to be gone now. He reached out and took her hand. It was cool to the touch, despite the warm room.

"I'm not angry, *Mammi*," he said. "It's probably better that Miriam know it all. The truth will set us free—isn't that what the Bible says?"

"*Yah*, it does." She smiled faintly.

"I don't feel like a good man, *Mammi*," he whispered.

"It isn't your feelings that matter," *Mammi* said, opening her eyes with a struggle. "You *are* a good man. It's a fact. You can trust me, dear one."

Amos looked up to see Miriam standing in the hallway, watching them with tears in her eyes. He gave Miriam a reassuring smile, and she turned away again.

"Do you think she'll stay?" *Mammi* asked.

"Here? With me?" he asked. He didn't have to ask who she meant. They both knew. Miriam was the one they were both thinking of tonight.

"*Yah*. She's your lawfully wedded wife, Amos."

"*Mammi…*" Amos swallowed. Must she push this? Must she force him to tell her the truth? "Miriam and I are very different people. Her understanding why I'm the way I am doesn't change *who* I am. Or who she is."

"I know…" *Mammi* sighed. "But you're such a good man, Amos. You have such a heart. I'd just hoped…"

And how Amos wished he could tell his grandmother otherwise and flood her old heart with joy. But it wasn't just for her joy that he wished he could say she was staying. Because having her here had been a relief in so many ways. He hadn't realized how much he'd missed his wife—even arguing with her! But that wasn't reason enough for her to stay. They had made mature and reasonable plans for their own futures. He looked up, but the hallway was empty.

"I'll be okay, *Mammi*," he whispered. "I will. I have Noah and Thomas and their families. I'm like a grandfather to those *kinner*."

"God's fingerprints are on everything," *Mammi* murmured, not seeming to be put off. "He's working still. Don't you doubt that. He's working…"

Mammi's eyes were still shut, and she breathed more slowly than seemed natural. Was she still holding out hope for his reunion with his wife? If only she'd give up, he wouldn't feel quite so guilty as he did. Miriam deserved a happy life, even if that meant she would live it away from him.

"Amos…" *Mammi*'s voice was quieter still. "Would you read me… John 14?"

Amos released *Mammi*'s hand and he wiped an errant tear from his cheek. These times sitting on the edge of his grandmother's bed, reading her Bible passages, had become so precious over the last weeks. He was sharing her hope—and oh, how he needed it tonight.

He picked up *Mammi*'s worn Bible, and he opened to the passage. She'd underlined the first few verses in pencil, and he started to read.

"'Let not your heart be troubled: ye believe in God, believe also in me. In my Father's house are many mansions: if it were not so, I would have told you. I go to prepare a place for you. And if I go and prepare a place for you, I will come again, and receive you unto myself; that where I am, there ye may be also...'"

He read slowly, enunciating the words the way she liked him to do, and then he paused, looking down at his grandmother's face. She still looked peaceful, and her eyes were shut, but something had changed. Her chest was still, and Amos could feel in his heart what had just happened.

Mammi was gone.

Amos stood up and went into the kitchen. Miriam was at the kitchen table, a cup of tea in front of her. She looked up as he came in.

"I think that...uh—" Amos looked helplessly toward Miriam. "I think that *Mammi* has passed away."

Miriam straightened, the blood seeping from her face. "What? When?"

"A few minutes ago, while I was reading the Bible to her," Amos said, and his voice broke.

Miriam went into the bedroom, and Amos stood immobile in the kitchen. She returned a couple of minutes later.

"Oh, Amos..." Miriam whispered, and she crossed the kitchen and stopped in front of him. "I'm so sorry..."

She stood there, her dark gaze meeting his with such deep sympathy that Amos felt the tears rise up in his eyes. His grandmother was gone, and his heart was full to breaking. He didn't know what to say, but Miriam saved him from trying to find it. She reached up and put her arms around his neck, tugging him down so that she could hold him. He slipped his arms around her waist and pulled her against him. He couldn't cry, though. While his throat was tight with unshed tears, and his chest felt so full of emotion that it might crack right open, he couldn't let it out.

Somehow, he'd been putting off feeling this impending loss—focusing on Miriam's presence, on his work, on the silly battles he and his wife always seemed to wage against each other. And maybe it had all been a way to avoid the heartbreaking truth that his beloved *mammi* had been dying. But there was no way to avoid it any longer.

Miriam cried in his arms, her tears soaking into his shirt. Having Miriam here, so close, was the most comforting thing he could imagine right now. *Mammi* had been right. And maybe she had been meddling in his life, hoping to make a reunion happen that really had no hope, but she had been right that having his wife here with him during his grandmother's death was exactly what he'd needed.

Even at the last, *Mammi* had been thinking of him…

Amos pulled back and Miriam wiped tears from her cheeks.

"We should call the doctor," Amos said woodenly.

"Yah." Miriam pulled a slip of paper out of her apron with the doctor's number on it. "And we need to let people know so that the funeral arrangements can begin…"

"Miriam—" He caught her hand. "Will you stay for the funeral?"

Because he couldn't face the thought of her leaving. Not yet.

"Of course," she said, and her chin trembled. "I promised *Mammi* I'd get you through it."

And perhaps he needed to get her through it, too. *Mammi* had meant so much to all of them, and Miriam had always had a special place in *Mammi*'s heart, even after the miserable breakup, after the community had judged her, and Amos did his best to forget her. Miriam deserved to mourn for *Mammi*, too.

But after the funeral, Miriam would go home. It had been the plan all along. Maybe it was best to simply be thankful for the time they'd had together, for this chance to truly connect as two human beings. *Mammi* had wanted them to get back together, and Amos had started to hope for the same impossible thing.

Gott, thank You that Miriam's here today...

That was all he could think to pray.

The funeral was put together by the community. *Mammi*'s friends and extended family worked in unison on the preparations so that Amos and Miriam had very little to do. Amos went through some of *Mammi*'s things—she didn't have much. There were some dresses, some *kapps* and aprons, an unfinished needlework project of a Bible verse and a box of little collectible animal figurines she'd bought over the years when she and *Dawdie* would travel together.

Noah and Thomas came by the house early to help Amos carry *Mammi*'s bed and the chest of drawers back upstairs to her bedroom. Miriam swept out the room, mopped it, wiped down the surfaces, and they moved the couch and chairs back to where they belonged. It felt suddenly very empty in that sitting room, and very, very lonely.

Mammi was buried in the community graveyard, and there were sermons, singing, a large meal put together at Amos's house that everyone contributed to.

The songs they sang were about Heaven, and their hope of eternity with *Gott*. Miriam had stood on the women's side, and Amos had stood shoulder to shoulder with Noah and Thomas on either side of him. The family from Ohio and Indiana had come, too, but when he looked up, it was Miriam's steady gaze that gave him the most strength. Whatever happened during wedding vows, while they didn't seem to guarantee happiness or a peaceful home, they did connect a man and a woman in an undeniable way.

Mammi's funeral was long, as all Amish funerals were. Amish funerals gave people time to accept the loss, and to hold the sadness in their hearts together. Mourning took time, and so did comfort. That was part of the Amish way—they took their time to do things properly, to feel them deeply. They didn't rush. Grieving was never done alone when one had a community like Redemption.

"She was the only grandmother I knew," Noah told Amos sadly, his infant son in his arms. "And she was so full of wisdom and hope."

"Yah..." Amos nodded. "She was very loved."

His mind kept going back to her final day—the one spent outdoors where she insisted that she was feeling better, and she kept telling stories. He knew that *Mammi*'s life hadn't been perfect. She'd buried her only adult son after that one terrible winter, but it could be argued that she'd lost him years before to addiction. She'd lost babies and had never had the house full of children she'd prayed for. *Mammi* had spent a lifetime praying, and not always seeing the results. Her life wasn't perfect, but somehow, when *Mammi* was looking back on her lifetime, she saw sweetness and beauty because she'd had her dear husband at her side.

The funeral passed by in a blur, and when the funeral day was done, and all the baking and casseroles had been left in his kitchen by kind neighbors, Amos knew that life would start to return to normal in degrees.

And he felt that his goodbye to his grandmother had been complete.

The next morning, Miriam stood in the kitchen dishing up bowls of oatmeal. After Amos had gone out to do his chores, Miriam had stripped the guest room bed, remade it with fresh sheets and swept the floor so that the room was as neat as she'd found it.

This house, so familiar, was not hers. This wasn't her home, even if she was starting to feel like she might have some claim to it after all they'd been through these last two weeks. It was almost like the honeymoon period after their wedding, when she felt that powerful tie to the man she'd vowed to love. And here she was, feeling that too-strong claim on Amos and this home, all over again.

Miriam was the one who kept feeling too much, needing too much. If she were just like the other women, she could quietly find contentment in keeping her home and supporting her husband. But Miriam wasn't like the others, and she'd grown to accept that. She wasn't the wife Amos needed. And this life in his home as his wife, as beautiful as it could be, wouldn't be enough for her. It was better to leave now, and deal with the heartbreak all at once. Because if she stayed longer, when she left they'd both be bitter and angry, and that would be worse.

Amos's boots resounded on the steps outside, and the door opened. She listened as his boots thunked to the floor and the water turned on for him to wash his hands.

"Good morning," he said, appearing in the mudroom doorway.

"Good morning," she replied, but the words felt tight in her throat.

"It felt good to get outside," Amos said. "It seems to help."

Miriam nodded. It likely did help, but she'd be outside soon enough when they were on their way to the bus depot. And then there would be a two-hour bus ride where she'd be holding back tears, and when she finally did get back outside again in Edson, she would find somewhere private, and those tears would fall.

But not until then... Amos might be looking for relief right here and right now, but her relief would have to wait.

"Breakfast smells good," Amos said, but as the words came out, his gaze landed on her travel bag, and he froze. He looked up at her, his eyebrows climbing. "You're leaving today?"

She hadn't meant to ask for the ride quite like this, although how she saw that going, she wasn't sure.

"If you'll drop me off at the bus station on your way into work," she said. "I've made us breakfast, and you have enough baking and extra food here to last you a month—" She forced a smile. "I think you'll be in good hands."

Just not hers. And that tugged at her heart. There had been other hands to show him compassion and care for the last ten years. Why should this hurt more now? He glanced over at the food on the counter—bags of muffins, loaves of bread, piles of produce.

"I thought you might stay a few days longer," he said, turning back to her.

"I'd only sit in this house alone," Miriam said, and she shook her head. "I don't think I could handle that."

"I like having you here," he whispered. "I like coming home to your cooking, and hearing your voice around the house."

"I've missed you, too, Amos," Miriam said. "But we have to be realistic now."

"Realistic," he said hollowly.

"Yah!" Was he going to force her to do this? "Amos, the longer I stay, the harder it is for me to go—"

Amos crossed the kitchen and he tugged her solidly into his arms. His lips came down over hers, and for what felt like a blessed eternity, he kissed her.

Amos pulled back, and Miriam sucked in a wavering breath. She wanted him to kiss her again, to let her forget that her bag was waiting...

"Don't go yet," Amos whispered.

Her heart squeezed in response. "Amos, don't do this to me…"

"Do what?" he asked, shaking his head. "I'm just asking you to stay a little longer."

"Why?" she asked helplessly. "What is there to be gained?"

"Maybe we could have some time to figure this out," he said hopefully.

"We went through all of this ten years ago!" she said, her voice starting to rise. "We figured it out then, Amos!"

Amos's dark gaze met hers solemnly. He'd always been so noble, so calm… "We could change our minds, you know. You could stay here. We could make a life together—try again."

"You don't really want that," she said.

Because she hadn't changed—she was the same woman who drove him crazy.

"Maybe I do," he replied.

"You say you do," she countered. "But what you want is to come home to me. You want me here, keeping your home, cooking your food, spending the evening together reading *The Budget*. You don't want the reality of what having me here would actually be!"

"It could be just like you described," he said. "We could vow to stop arguing."

"It didn't work," she said. "Not even for *Mammi*. This doesn't come naturally to either of us. Why can't you see me for who I am, Amos? I wouldn't be a patient and meek wife, waiting for you to figure out the radio ads. I'd go find out how to do them myself! And put together some ideas, and even make a budget for it," she said. "I'd want a hand in your business. I'd want to run it *together*."

He pressed his lips together in a look she recognized.

"I can see the look on your face," Miriam went on. "You don't want that life, but that's who I am. I've got a strip mall that will provide some income, and I've got ideas for that other shop, too. It's not like other women don't run businesses!"

"Other women do it with less ferocity," he said with a small smile.

"I'm not like them!" Miriam rubbed her hands over her face. Talking about this more wasn't going to change anything. Letting her emotions out wasn't going to help.

"Why can't you just stay a little while?" Amos asked quietly. "I'm not asking for forever yet. I'm just asking you to stay with me…see if you might like it—"

"No!" The tears Miriam had been working so hard to hold back started to flow.

"Why?" he demanded, his own agonized gaze locked on to hers. "Give me a good reason why not, Miriam! You're my *wife*!"

"Because we've done this before!" she sobbed. "We've done it, and it tore me into pieces when I had to leave! And it'll only be worse this time!"

"Worse?" He threw his hands in the air. "How on earth could it be worse?"

"Because *I love you*!" The words came out before she could think better of them, and Amos suddenly stilled, his expression shocked. But she did…she was only really realizing it now. That's why her heart kept pulling toward him. It was why she kept falling into his arms, and why he could hurt her like no other. She loved him.

She'd fallen in love with her husband, and it wouldn't help them one bit. Loving a man didn't make a relationship work! Loving him only made it more painful when they hurt each other.

"Yah..." she breathed. "I love you. And I shouldn't... I'm not what you need, and I can't change who I am. If I don't go home now, I'm not sure I'll survive this. You *have* to let me go!"

Chapter Twelve

Amos stared at Miriam, his heart lodged in his throat. She *loved* him? After all these years of wondering if she ever had, now she loved him? Her eyes sparkled with unshed tears, and a tendril of hair had fallen loose from her *kapp*. She was petite next to him, and all of that pent-up energy inside of her usually made her seem taller than she really was. She used to intimidate him, if he had to be brutally honest. But right now, looking into her eyes, looking for answers to that way his heart was yearning toward her, she didn't look any bigger than life anymore. She looked fragile.

"Miriam—" His voice caught.

Miriam shook her head. "Don't make it harder, Amos."

"What do you think I'll say?" he asked.

"You'll tell me that I'm being foolish. That what I'm feeling is connected to a death of someone we both cared about. That given some time, I'll get my footing back, and—"

"Seriously?" Amos asked. "You think that's what I'd say when you tell me that you love me?"

"It's what you should say." She swallowed.

And maybe it was. Maybe that would help them both get past this, but it wasn't what he felt. He'd been running from this for ten years, but he'd never said the words to her before.

"I love you, too," he said, and he caught her slim hand in his calloused grip, looking down into her tearstained face.

"You don't have to say that—" she started.

"Miriam, stop it!" he said, and he shook his head. "I love you! Okay? I'm not saying what I think is appropriate. I'm telling you how I feel. I think about you constantly. I have for the entire time you were gone. It would be easier not to love you! Much easier. Because you're leaving again, and I'm going to be left alone in this house trying to hold on to some little detail—like the way you smell so soft and sweet, or the sound of your laugh. But I'll forget—ever so slowly, it will slip away, and that feeling of forgetting will be worse than torturing myself with memories. So this isn't convenient for me, either."

Amos tugged her close, his gaze locked on to hers. For a moment, he wasn't sure what to do, but then he slid his arms around her waist and lowered his lips over hers. Miriam rose up onto the tips of her toes to meet his kiss. She wasn't what he needed, and he wasn't the kind of man who completed her, either. But his heart didn't want to listen to reason. He wanted to hold her close and kiss her senseless, and never think ahead to the future when they'd inevitably break each other's hearts all over again.

If Amos couldn't love his own wife, then who could he love? There was no moving on for an Amish couple. They were married until death parted them, and he couldn't look for another woman who might be a better fit. When he'd promised to be hers ten years ago, he had signed his entire future into her hands.

Miriam pulled back first, and Amos looked down at her plump lips. She was so beautiful…but she wasn't truly his.

"I'm not what you need," she repeated. "And that matters. If *Mammi* showed me anything, it was that you're a good man with a tender heart. There is nothing wrong with you wanting a wife at home who will trust the business to your capable hands. Nothing! But I'm not that woman. You don't want all of this energy focused on you and your business," Miriam said. "Just accept that. And we can go about our separate ways. And if we're ever in trouble—if one of us is sick or hurt, or in need of help—"

"I'll be here," he said, his voice low and deep. "Always."

"And I'll take care of you," she said earnestly. "If you need me, all you need to do is send me a message and I'll drop everything. You still have a wife. You'll appreciate me more if you see less of me."

Did she feel the same about him? Was he easier to appreciate when she saw him once a decade? Were they better supporting each other through the hard times, and then taking their distance again?

Miriam took a purposeful step away from him,

dropped her gaze and wiped her face. Then she walked toward her bag and picked it up. She hadn't noticed the hair that had come loose, and when she looked back at him, she looked bedraggled and sorrowful.

"Would you drive me to the bus station, Amos?" she asked quietly. "I need to get home."

Her voice caught at the last word: *home.*

This was her home, and Amos wanted to shout it at her, to make her hear it! *He* was supposed to be her home—his arms were supposed to be her protection. But whatever marriage was supposed to be, they'd always seemed to miss the mark.

"If that's what you want," he said, and he caught her eye, waiting for her to see what she was so determined to walk away from. "If it's what you really, truly want."

Would she change her mind?

"Thank you, Amos," she whispered. "I appreciate it."

No, she wouldn't. She always had been stronger than him in spirit. She was tougher, more determined, more convinced of her own views. No one changed Miriam Lapp's mind on anything.

Amos let out a slow breath and nodded. He'd watched his mother be miserable trying to make his father happy. He'd watched her deny herself of the things she needed most desperately, just to try and please her husband. And maybe medication wasn't the same thing as what was most necessary to Miriam's happiness, but regardless, Amos would never do that to his wife. Amos wouldn't beg her to come back, or change herself, or to give up one fraction of the life she longed for. Not for him.

He went outside and hitched up the buggy. As he

worked, he wondered if Miriam weren't right. This was painful now, but she was right that they were so very different. They wanted different things from life, from marriage, from love... And when Miriam was happy and bright, shimmering with energy, that was when she was meddling in his business, giving him unasked for advice or staring down one of his customers.

She didn't want to be a wife at home, trusting her husband to provide. She wanted to be pushing him forward, making him better, putting her fingerprints all over the business he'd built up from scratch. She was so much energy, so much good intention, so much forward motion...

They drove each other crazy.

Gott, *how did we get here?* he prayed in his heart. *How did we end up loving each other, but completely incapable of living together?*

No one would understand this if he tried to explain. Noah and Thomas would nod, and then exchange perplexed looks with each other. *Mammi* was the only one who came close to understanding the complexity of his relationship with his wife, but even she had been bent on trying to reunite them.

Amos brought the buggy to the side of the house, and then took her travel bag and put it in the back. Miriam didn't wait for a hand up. She settled herself on the bench, and he went around to the other side.

He'd drive his wife to the bus station, and then he'd have to let her go.

She was right. If they did this later—in a month or two, in another year—it just might tear out his heart, too, and he couldn't be sure he'd recover.

* * *

When the bus pulled away from the station, Amos couldn't see Miriam's face. All he could make out was the white of her *kapp*, and then just as the bus came past him, he got a flash of her face, and her hand suddenly pressed against the glass.

He stood there as the bus rumbled away, his heart hovering in his chest as if it was afraid to beat again.

She was gone.

He suddenly remembered that carved box. He'd finished it the night before, and he'd forgotten to give it to her. Even in their goodbyes, he seemed to be messing this up.

He swallowed hard and turned back toward the station. His horse and buggy waited in the parking lot, and he pushed past an Amish man he knew, refusing to look up. He couldn't face friendly banter right now. He couldn't pretend he was fine when inside of him he was falling apart.

When he got to the buggy, he hoisted himself up into the seat, his vision blurred by unshed tears. They wouldn't fall, but they hung there in front of his eyes, making it impossible to see anything clearly.

His shop was waiting for him. Thomas and Noah would be starting to worry…

He'd go back to work. He'd pour this heartache into his craft, and he'd work long hours so that when he got back to his empty house, he could simply drop into bed and melt into the oblivion of sleep.

His heart would heal…eventually. And *Gott* would give him something else to live for. Before, it was Thomas and Noah who came into his life. Maybe there would be someone else who would need his battered heart and his best intentions.

Just not a wife.

Life was long, and as *Mammi* always said, *Gott* worked in the details. *Gott* still had something for him to do, a way for him to brighten his corner. He'd just have to wait for the Almighty to put it in his path.

Gott might be preparing mansions for them in Heaven, but He didn't forget his *kinner* on earth, either.

Miriam carried her bag into the family farmhouse. The Schwartz farm was large, even by Amish standards. The house had seven bedrooms, and a summer kitchen that extended off the south end for cooler summer cooking. Japheth's wife, Arleta, was peeling potatoes into a large pot, and she looked up with a tired smile.

"You're back," Arleta said.

"*Yah*, I'm back." Miriam set down her bag.

"Your brother thought you might stay with your husband," Arleta said. "I confess, I thought you might, too."

Miriam shook her head. "I only stayed as long as I did because Amos's grandmother needed my help in her final days."

"*Yah*, I'm sorry for your loss," Arleta said. "I know you loved her. What with your father's passing, and now Mary Lapp—"

Miriam nodded. "It's been a hard season."

Miriam glanced around the wide kitchen. The table seated twelve, easily, and there was space enough for a row of storage cabinets that held bulk ingredients.

Once upon a time, this house had been full of extended family and visiting friends filling up all this extra space, and now it was Japheth's family, his wife and four children. Her brother was nowhere to be seen, and she wondered if he was in his office, or away from the house. She pulled out the envelope that held the documents she needed to prove that she owned the strip mall. This was her most important task right now.

Overhead, Miriam could hear one of her nieces sweeping, and out the kitchen window two more of her nieces were bent over in the garden, weeding. The baby was in a cradle in the corner of the kitchen, and Arleta was pregnant again. She'd had no trouble with childbearing.

"It might be a good time to reconnect with Amos…" Arleta said hesitantly, and Miriam's mind was tugged back to her sister-in-law.

"Are you anxious to get rid of me?" Miriam asked with an uncomfortable laugh.

"Of course not." Arleta shook her head. "But I really think your father did you wrong by meddling in your marriage the way he did, and your brother and I never agreed with that. We couldn't counter him, of course. That would have been wrong. But Amos Lapp is a good man. He might not be as successful as we are, but he's still a good man. I'm sure you don't want to be keeping house with me. I mean, I'm good company, but I'm not enough." Arleta shot her a teasing smile.

That was what most everyone would assume—that Miriam had finally gone home to her husband. But it wasn't an option.

"I won't be getting in your way," Miriam said. "I found the documents I went to look for. My *daet* signed a certain property over to me, and I'm going to use that income to start a new business that I can run."

"Which property?" Arleta's tone sharpened.

"The strip mall on Main Street," Miriam said.

"Hmm." Arleta turned back to the potato peeling, but her movements were sharper now, and the peels whisked into a bucket.

"What did I say?" Miriam asked.

Was Arleta angry at her getting even that much? Arleta stopped peeling and looked up.

"And you think that's the right move for you?" her sister-in-law asked pointedly. "You think you should run a business and forget about keeping a home?"

Miriam glanced around the spotless kitchen. This *was* her home. She'd been born in this house.

"Do you want me underfoot?" Miriam asked.

"I'm not asking you to leave if you're determined to stay. We all have to choose the life we want, and if this is it, then who am I to argue with you? But this is a big house!" Arleta said. "There's enough work to share! My girls and I can keep it running, but we have a whole garden we let go to seed because we don't have enough time in the day to take care of it! And you want to go start your business like you're some child playing games with her *daet*. And Japheth doesn't need the help, if you're thinking of working with him! He's the man. He can keep it running. No one wants a woman coming to them for lease payments, anyway. Your father spoiled you! He let you play like a little girl, going with him to take care of business when you should have been here at the house doing your duty. Let Japheth take care of the men's work. What about doing the work you're *sup-*

posed to be doing? If you won't do it for your husband, you can do it here."

Miriam stared at her sister-in-law in surprise. She hadn't realized that all this bitterness was under the surface. When her *daet* was alive, he ruled this house and he dictated that Miriam should go with him to understand the business. Miriam had pitched in when she was at home, but that wasn't the majority of her day.

"My *daet* gave me that business," Miriam said, her voice tight. "And I will need it to provide for myself. Maybe I'll end up getting a little place of my own—"

"You have a husband to provide for you," Arleta said. "You have a home with him. I don't know why you refuse to go back."

"Because I don't make my husband happy!" she blurted out, tears springing to her eyes.

Behind her, Japheth's voice reverberated. "Should I go have a word with him? I don't care if he's happy or not! You're his wife!"

Miriam turned to see her brother in the doorway. Japheth stood there with his arms crossed over his chest, his eyes ablaze. He didn't have his hat on inside, and his hair was slightly askew.

"No, I don't need you to go shout at Amos," she snapped. "I'm perfectly capable of speaking for myself. Amos and I understand each other very well. We're just…different."

"As are all men and women!" Japheth retorted. "Miriam, our *daet* didn't do you any favors by chasing away your husband. I'll tell you that much. I thought if you went back to see Amos, you'd see reason, too."

"*Daet* didn't chase him away…" she said. "If anyone had ruined things, it was me and Amos. We were adult enough to make a marriage work or tear it apart."

"*Yah, Daet* did," Japheth replied resolutely. "*Daet* made you into the son he always wanted, and that didn't prepare you for married life."

Miriam exchanged a tired look with her brother. This was an old conversation. Their father had taken more interest in teaching Miriam the business because she'd caught on to it more quickly. It was second nature to her. The numbers came easily, the equations made sense. And she had an instinct for what would make a business work that Japheth had always lacked. Their *daet* had been so very proud of Miriam's ability…just not proud enough to leave her a proper inheritance.

"Japheth, I can't apologize for who I am," Miriam said. "I'm tired of doing that."

Japheth rubbed a hand over his thinning hair. "Come to my office. Since you're here, I need you to look at some ledgers for me. I can't make sense of them."

"Arleta needs help here," Miriam said.

"She's fine. Come on." He started out of the room and Miriam cast her sister-in-law an apologetic look. "Your husband might not need your business sense, but right now I do."

"I was hoping she could help me with that garden," Arleta said, raising her voice after Japheth, and there was a tension in her voice that meant Japheth and Arleta had discussed this before.

"I *will* help you with it, Arleta," Miriam said. "I'm sorry I didn't help more before. I'll do better. I'll get started this evening, in fact."

Maybe some hard work would help to distract her from her own heartbreak today.

Miriam followed her brother down the hallway to the office that used to be their father's. She paused at the door as Japheth went inside. He moved easily around the room, confident in his new ownership, it seemed.

"How long has Arleta been upset with me?" Miriam asked.

"What?" Japheth shook his head. "She's fine."

"She's not fine," Miriam replied. "She's angry."

Japheth sighed. "You have to see that it wasn't fair the way *Daet* treated you. If *Daet* had given me half the tutoring he gave you, I'd be more ready to do this."

"He let you run a couple of businesses," she countered.

"But he showed you how to run all of them at once," her brother replied.

"I don't think he expected to die so soon," Miriam said.

"True." Japheth met her gaze. "So we have to talk about this seriously. I know that Arleta wants your help around the house, but I'm going to need some help with running things until I get a better handle on all the properties."

The prospect of staying involved with the business should spark some excitement in her. She paused, waiting to feel something, but she couldn't quite summon up the enthusiasm. She was emotionally empty.

"Okay," she said after a beat of silence.

"I'll need you to show me what *Daet* taught you," he said. "Maybe you could come around with me to the different properties. But don't say anything in front of people. We'll talk about it in the buggy."

The same thing Amos had asked of her—help out, give her opinion and let the man look like the one who had thought of it all. When could she take the credit?

"I can do that," she said. It didn't matter, anyway.

"I can help you with the strip mall," he added. "The renters might respond better to a man. *Daet* was pretty tough, and that kept things orderly."

"I don't need help with it," she replied.

Japheth shrugged. "That's fine. I wanted to take Arleta to see some of her family in Indiana. If you'll be here, maybe you could take care of things with the businesses while we're away. That would be helpful…"

Things would continue as they had with *Daet*. She'd pitch in, offer her advice, scan the ledgers for inaccuracies and look for ways to improve the efficiency. It had been exciting when *Daet* was alive—but helping her brother would be a different dynamic. She would no longer be the daughter learning, she'd be the sister teaching. This was a chance to prove herself, and if her brother would be willing to accept her input in the running of things, she could help to build the Schwartz legacy even further. Even if that legacy was almost entirely in her brother's name.

And yet, it wasn't quite as exciting anymore, and she couldn't put her finger on why. Was it that she'd gotten a glimpse of another life…one she thought she didn't want…?

"Miriam?" Japheth said, softening his voice. "Are you okay?"

A tear had slipped down her cheek, and she hastily wiped it away. "*Yah*. I miss him…"

"Me, too. It's not the same coming into this office and not having *Daet* tell me to stop messing with his filing system." Japheth smiled sadly and put his hand on a stack of invoices yet to be filed.

But her brother had misunderstood. While she did miss *Daet* dearly, it was Amos her heart was aching for.

She'd known there would be a cost to staying in Redemption for as long as she did, and she was paying it now. Would she stop loving Amos over time, or would she just learn to live with this ache of loss? She wasn't sure. But walking away from Amos this time was the hardest thing she'd ever done.

Chapter Thirteen

The visit with the adoption agent was more productive than Thomas had dared to hope, and Amos and Noah were incredibly happy for Thomas and Patience. If *Mammi* had only been able to see their prayer answered, because Thomas and Patience were adopting a little boy. The process had moved more quickly than any of them had expected, and tonight a two-year-old child was being introduced to his new, adoptive family for the first time.

Amos gave his horse a last stroke down his long nose before he headed out of Thomas Wiebe's stable for the house.

There was a minivan in the drive, so it appeared that the adoption agent was still there. Thomas had asked Amos to come that evening and meet their new son, and he wondered if he should have come a little later…given the family more time alone before coming to say hello. He'd assumed that Noah would be there, too, and their mother, Rachel. But there were no extra buggies. Not yet at least. Maybe they were on their way.

Amos had had a lot of invitations to dinner over the last few days from families in their community. With *Mammi*'s passing, the community had pulled together to not only keep his kitchen stocked during his time of grief, but to make sure he wasn't lonesome, either. But it wasn't friends and extended family who he was missing most right now.

He was missing his wife. It was supposed to get easier without her—it hadn't.

Amos headed up the side steps and he pushed the screen door open. He could see Thomas and Patience at the kitchen table with an Englisher woman who looked to be in her forties. As he came all the way in, he spotted Rue sitting cross-legged on the floor with a toddler next to her. The little boy held a blanket that appeared to have a cartoon mouse on the front of it—very un-Amish. Rue reached forward and smoothed a hand down his hair lovingly. The little boy leaned toward her, and Rue wrapped her thin arms around him tenderly. Amos couldn't help but smile.

That little boy had just found the most loving home imaginable, and he had no idea yet how blessed he was.

"Amos, you made it!" Thomas said. "Come in, come in."

Amos glanced around. The adoption agent, deep in conversation with Patience, was a middle-aged woman wearing a pantsuit. She was plump and looked pleasant enough.

"I feel like I misunderstood an invitation?" Amos said uncertainly.

"Not at all," Patience said, looking up. "We invited

you purposefully. That's Cruise, over there, getting to know his new sister."

Amos smiled wistfully. "He's really cute."

"He's got a Mickey Mouse blanket!" Rue said. "He loves it a lot."

"And he will keep it for as long as he wants," Thomas said, perhaps a little more firmly than necessary. "We're just so glad to bring him into our family. Rue seems to be his favorite so far."

"That's a wonderful sign actually," the Englisher woman said. "Oftentimes, the sibling relationships can be the toughest. I'm glad your daughter is so open to having a little brother."

"Oh, I was praying for a brother," Rue said with a wide smile. "And sometimes *Gott* doesn't give you the one you think you'll get. Sometimes he's got a brother waiting somewhere else. And Cruise is *wonderful.*"

Cruise—a very un-Amish name, too, but no one in this room seemed to mind a bit, least of all Amos. Thomas was getting a son tonight, and Amos's heart was full of joy on his behalf.

"This is Nancy Cross," Patience said, pulling his attention back. "She's an adoption agent. When we talked to her last time, she had mentioned a rather special situation, and we thought of you right away."

Patience's gaze moved toward Cruise on the floor. She slipped away from the table and went over to where the *kinner* were playing. As she crouched down next to them, she ran a protective hand over the toddler's wispy blond hair.

"You thought of me?" Amos pulled up a chair and sank into it.

"I'll just let Nancy explain," Thomas said.

"Hello, Mr. Lapp," the woman said with a warm smile. She offered him her hand, and he shook it.

"Just Amos is fine," Amos said. "Nice to meet you."

"Likewise," Nancy said. "When we were doing our adoption interview, Thomas told us about how you took him and his brother into your home and raised them like they were your own. It was a really touching story, and I was moved, truly."

Amos smiled awkwardly. "I was more than happy to do it."

"Well, I wanted to tell you a story about four boys," Nancy said, pulling out a file folder and removing some color school photos. "This is Michael, Jack, Vince and Colby. Their parents were killed in a car accident six months ago, and boys this age can be hard to place separately, let alone together. These brothers need a stable home and they need to stay together. They were raised Mennonite, but they don't have any extended family to take them in. They're in different foster homes right now, and it's stressful for them."

Amos looked down at the last photo of the boys together. The tallest boy looked like he might shave already. The younger boys all looked similar—the same curls and big, brown eyes.

"That was taken just before they went into foster care," Nancy added.

It was the sadness in their faces that tugged at him the most. He looked over to where Patience crouched next to Rue. She held her arms out to Cruise, but the toddler leaned toward Rue instead. She let her hands drop, but her face showed that she had the ability to wait and win the little boy over. She sank down all the way onto the floor, tucking her legs underneath her.

"And you want me to be their new home," Amos surmised.

"Well, sir," Nancy said. "We were hoping you'd consider it. It takes a really special person to be able to raise boys well, to love them, to make them feel secure. And these boys need that badly. I don't mean to pressure you in any way. I just wanted to let you think it over."

Four boys who needed a *daet* and a home... The last time he'd done this, he'd had *Mammi* to help him out, to be the woman in the home, to cook the meals and mend the clothes...

"It's a big responsibility," he agreed.

"This is my card," Nancy said, passing it over and rising to her feet. "If you are interested, please give me a call. But again, no pressure."

"*Yah.* I'll think it over..." He put his finger on the photo. "Could I keep that?"

He shouldn't. The Amish didn't have photos in their homes, but somehow he wondered if Gott would forgive him this little lapse... It was a very unique circumstance.

Nancy smiled. "Absolutely. You can keep all of the photos if you like—"

"No, just one." He pulled the photo closer and then gave her a smile. "I'll pray on it."

Nancy said her goodbyes, shook hands with Thomas and Patience and then she took her leave. Amos stood up then, too.

"I'll let you have some privacy as a little family," Amos said.

"You're part of the family," Thomas said. "And you've got another grandson."

"I couldn't be happier," Amos said, and he leaned in and gave Thomas a hug and a slap on the back.

"Let me help you with your buggy," Thomas said.

The two men went outside together. The sun was starting to set, but it was still light enough to be able to be able to work without a lantern.

"What do you think?" Thomas asked.

"About the boys?" Amos sucked in a slow breath. "I don't have *Mammi* here to help me out anymore. It wouldn't be quite the same."

"You've got all of us, though," Thomas said. "And you're not half-bad in the kitchen, you know."

Amos smiled sadly. *"Yah..."*

They brought the horse out to the buggy, and as the men hitched him back up, Amos looked toward the house. The kerosene lamp light inside made it so that he could see Patience in the window. She was standing and holding Cruise in her arms now. She smiled tenderly at him, and he stared at her, wide-eyed.

"Your wife is a wonderful woman," Amos said quietly. *"Gott* blessed you with her."

"Yah," Thomas agreed. "She makes me a better man, too. I don't know if you remember, but when Rue came to live with me, I took away her suitcase of Englisher clothes, and I just about broke her heart. With this little boy, we knew he had an Englisher name, and Patience warned me that he'd come with his own little treasures that comforted him. It was Patience who told me that he needed to keep his name and his treasures."

"You won't change his name?" Amos asked.

"No." Thomas shook his head. "His name was a gift from his biological mother, and we won't take that away. He'll be Cruise Wiebe, an Amish boy with a strange name, but we'll give him a middle name, though. I was thinking Amos would be nice."

"Really?" Amos looked at Thomas, stunned. "After me?"

"You're the father who taught me how to be an adoptive *daet*," Thomas said, and he dropped his gaze, rubbing a hand over his reddish beard.

"I'm honored," Amos murmured.

He looked down at the picture of the boys in his hand. "Did Patience really change you that much?"

"Yah…" Thomas shrugged. "But that's marriage, isn't it? We all become more flexible, and we're better for it." Thomas seemed to realize what he'd said, and he shot him an apologetic look. "I didn't mean—"

"No, no," Amos said. "It's fine."

"The thing is, I was a good man before her," Thomas said. "But I'm a better father with her…if that makes sense."

It did make sense. Because looking down at the photo of four boys so desperately in need of a home, Amos was sorely tempted to take them in. But he wasn't imagining doing this by himself anymore. In his mind's eye, Miriam was at his side, and they were raising a houseful of boys together.

He missed her desperately, but a life with Miriam would involve some considerable change on his part. He'd have to accept her influence in his home and in his business. And he had a feeling that Miriam could make him into a better version of himself, too, if he'd just be willing to let her past his defenses. Thomas was a better man with Patience, and a better father. And Miriam could do the same for him. He wasn't going to be so stubborn as to claim he couldn't improve.

Was he really considering this?

"You just made up your mind, didn't you?" Thomas said, eyeing him with a small smile.

"Yah " Amos shot Thomas a grin. "But it begins with a trip to Edson first thing in the morning."

Thomas's smile broadened. "I'll be praying you come home with Miriam."

"I need all the prayer I can get, Thomas," Amos said. "Now let me get home. You go on in to your family."

Miriam stood outside her strip mall with a pad of paper in one hand as she jotted down notes of things that needed to be improved over the next several months. One shop—a florist—had a water leak that hadn't been reported, and that would be a more expensive fix. She'd already had some firm words with the owner of the business about reporting these things promptly or having his lease canceled.

She didn't need her brother's help in delivering that kind of reprimand, and the leasees would simply have to get used to reporting to her. According to her records, they hadn't raised lease prices in the last five years, so she would revisit those numbers, but she didn't want to be unfair to the businesses there, either. She'd have to look at all the details first.

"Ma'am?" The florist came out of his shop, and he shot her an uncomfortable look. "I want to apologize for my attitude before. I shouldn't have argued with you, and I can promise that I'll be checking those hoses from now on."

"Thank you," Miriam said, and she softened her tone. "I appreciate that. We have a cell phone for emergency calls, so please only use it then. You can leave a message and we'll get the right people in to fix things like water leaks. Those can't be left."

"Right." The man nodded. "I'll do that."

He headed back into his shop, and she smiled faintly. She'd been called "ma'am." She liked the sound of it—even if it was rather fancy. Then her smile slipped. There was something Amos had said… *Do you want to live in a house with your brother, and have a sprawling network of businesses that call you "ma'am" like some Englisher woman?*

She'd have these people's respect, and within a matter of months, she'd have them giving her the same deference they'd given her father… She might have to find a little home to live in alone, though, if her sister-in-law didn't like the current arrangement. Japheth and Arleta would need a family home to themselves. Marriages oftentimes needed a bit of space… That was ironic, because her marriage seemed to need more than most!

"Whoa…"

Miriam looked up as her brother reined in his buggy, but she froze when she saw who was with him.

"Amos?" she breathed.

Her husband was already rising to his feet as the buggy came to a stop, and Amos jumped down and gave Japheth a nod of thanks, then he turned his drilling gaze onto her. Miriam smoothed her hands down the front of her dress.

"What are you doing here?" Miriam asked, and her voice trembled just a little more than she wanted it to.

Amos crossed the distance between them, and it was like everything around them disappeared.

"I missed you," he said softly.

"So you came to visit?" she asked feebly. Were they going to include this in their relationship now, too? Somehow, she couldn't complain.

"Not exactly," he said, and he caught her hand in his. She squeezed his fingers just as tightly in return. "I came to ask you to come home…"

Miriam blinked at him, and her gaze flickered over to where her brother still sat in the buggy, trying to pretend he wasn't watching.

"Did my brother ask you to do this?" she asked falteringly. "Because—"

"This is me," Amos said quietly. "I showed up at the house looking for you, and your brother said he'd give me a ride to find you."

"Oh…" she said faintly.

"Miriam, I love you," he said. "And I know you love me. I've been a fool. I wanted you to be someone else—to be meeker and quieter and less of everything that you are. But that was wrong. You're intelligent, and beautiful, and I want you to come home and be a part of everything."

"What?" She squinted up at him. "Amos, you can't mean that."

"Why not?" he asked.

"Because I drive you crazy!"

"*Yah*, sometimes." A smile flickered at the corners of

his lips. "But I need you. I need your help, and I think *Gott* is showing me just how much I need it."

"What changed?" she whispered.

"I missed you so much my whole chest hurt," he said. "I went to bed at night and missed you. I went to work and I missed you. I tried to pray and I missed you… I was starting to get the message that I needed you back at home with me, because I don't think getting over you is even an option." He swallowed, and his gaze met hers. "And then I got the chance to fill my home with *kinner*…"

"What?" she breathed.

"It's a little sudden," he said. "But in my experience, the best things seem to be."

He pulled out a photograph of four boys, and she looked at those sad faces and her heart nearly broke. They needed a mother…

"They need a home, and I've been asked if I would adopt them," Amos said. "I've got a bit of a track record with older kids because of Thomas and Noah. And, well… Thomas and Patience are adopting a little boy, and they heard about these *kinner*."

"You want to raise them?" she asked. "Is that what you're saying? You want to adopt these boys?"

"That's exactly what I'm saying. It would be a big job," he said. "They aren't Amish born, these boys. But I don't know… I look at those faces, and I think that I could offer them something—stability, faith, a real home. And for me…for us…it would be a chance at a house full of love and laughter."

"I'll still drive you crazy," she said, shaking her head.

"I'd still want to know about the business, and want to grow it in spite of you."

"Good." He nodded earnestly. "Good! Miriam, I'll need all your energy, and intuition, and business sense. Because if you and I adopt these boys, they'll take up a lot of time and dedication. If you'd be a wife to me, and a *mamm* to them, and…a manager at the shop…"

Miriam felt tears well in her eyes.

"Really?"

"Thomas said something that made me think. You have to bend for a wife. And the right woman can make you a better man."

Miriam was silent, and she fingered the photo of the boys. Her heart was already reaching toward them, and she sent up a prayer.

Gott, *is this Your will? Can I go home now?*

"You haven't contacted anyone about the radio ad, have you?" she asked with a teary smile.

"Not yet," Amos admitted. "I'm not great with that stuff. But you and I together, Miriam, we could do this… If you wanted to."

"I've missed you," she whispered.

Amos bent down and covered her lips with his. His kiss was soft and enveloping. When he finally pulled back, he murmured, "Come home with me…"

She nodded. "I'll have to help my brother a little bit, though."

"I'll be willing to share your expertise, Miriam," Japheth called from the buggy, and she laughed softly at her brother's grin. Had he heard all of that?

"*Yah*, Amos," Miriam said, looking up into her husband's hopeful face. "I'll come home with you, and I'll be a wife to you, and we'll adopt those boys together."

Because it felt right. In her heart, she could feel *Gott*'s smile on this.

She'd be a *mamm*… It hardly seemed real, and as she looked down at the photo again, she felt her heart open just a little bit wider. Yes, she'd be a *mamm*!

Amos slid an arm around her, and she tipped her head onto his shoulder. She knew exactly where her home was, and it wasn't here in Edson any longer—it was wherever her husband happened to be.

Mammi had been right, after all, it seemed. *Gott* had been working.

Epilogue

On a chilly morning in September, when the leaves were just starting to turn yellow on the trees outside, when the mornings were getting cooler, and the garden was turning brown outside the kitchen window, Miriam tucked a package of banana bread into the last lunch bag and handed it to Michael. He was the oldest, and he stood there—broad shoulders, a dusting of a mustache on his upper lip. Michael had been the hardest to reach the last couple of months. He'd been so quiet and stoic... almost like there was Amish inside of him, after all.

"I think you'll like your lunch, Michael," Miriam said, casting him a smile. "I'm giving you a little extra—growing boys need to eat."

The boys all wore their new school clothes—store-bought pants and suspenders, and hand-sewn shirts that Miriam had made herself in the evenings since they'd arrived in their home. Several women from the community, including Natasha Zook, came over to sew with her to get the boys ready for school that fall. And they each had four fresh new shirts, and three pairs of pants to last them the winter. If they didn't get torn... Boys tended to wear out clothes before they outgrew them—at least, that was the advice she'd received from Fannie Mast. And Fannie would know.

The last few months Miriam had been feeding her new sons food they loved, food they'd never tried before, and discovering their favorites. Babies bonded with milk, but big boys like these needed shoofly pie and fried chicken. A *mamm* fed her boys—and she'd been reveling in this new role of wife and mother.

Outside, Amos had just hitched the buggy, and the horses shifted their hooves impatiently. Miriam glanced out the window at Amos, who was leaning forward, waiting for them.

"Are you ready for your first day at school?" Miriam asked brightly.

"We don't know Dutch," Jack, who was twelve, said nervously. He'd been mentioning the same thing over and over for weeks. It was his personal worry.

"That's okay," Miriam said for the hundredth time, it felt like. "The teacher understands. You'll be fine. And you'll meet some other *kinner* your age—" She paused, winced. "Kids your age," she amended. "And you'll be back home before you know it. I'll make sure there are some warm cookies, if that helps."

"Okay." Jack smiled faintly. He still looked nervous.

Vince was ten, and he peeked into his cloth lunch bag, rooting around. Michael nudged him.

"Wait until lunch, Vince," he said.

"I was only looking..." And Vince glanced up at Miriam with a small smile. They all knew Miriam well enough by now to know that she wouldn't get upset over them eating. If anything, Miriam took great joy in feeding these growing boys. *Her boys.* Her heart flooded with love just looking at them.

"All right," Miriam said. "Off you go. *Daet* is waiting. Have a good day."

The boys seemed okay with Dutch names for *mom* and *dad*, because they were different enough not to overlap with their memories of their birth parents. But just sending them off today…it didn't feel quite right.

Michael opened the front door, but before he could push open the screen, Miriam said, "Boys!"

They turned, and her heart sped up. She wasn't used to making speeches, but before they went out the door to school for the first time, she felt like she needed to say something important.

"Boys, I want you to remember something," Miriam said earnestly. "I love you all. I know this is different and new, and I know we'll all stumble a little while we figure out how to be a family, but one thing you'll learn about me is that I'm very stubborn. I might drive you a little crazy with it sometimes, but the good part about me is that nothing you do will ever shake my love for you. Ever. I'm just too stubborn to change my mind once it's set, and I love you. Do you understand? I'm your *mamm* now, and I will love you until the end of time. That's how this works."

It hadn't been quite what she wanted to say, but it would do.

Colby, who was the youngest at nine years old, came back into the kitchen and wrapped his arms around her waist in a tight hug. She put a hand on the top of his hat on his head, and then he headed back to the door as quickly as he'd hugged her.

"Bye, *Mamm*," Colby said. "See you after school."

Michael shot her a shy smile, then opened the screen, and the boys all tramped outside toward the buggy where Amos waited.

This was it—their first day of school. And they were plenty old enough to handle it just fine, so why was she feeling this strange flutter of anxiety at the thought of it? Maybe this was just part of being a *mamm*.

Amos smiled over their heads at her. He'd drive the boys to school for the first day, and they'd walk home. It wasn't far, but the first day seemed like an important day to get a ride with their new *daet*.

Amos's smile warmed his eyes and made her cheeks grow warm in response.

"Have a good day at work, Amos!" she called.

"Yah." He blew her a kiss. "You're coming by the shop later, right?"

"I'll be there!"

Then Amos flicked the reins and they were off.

Miriam watched the buggy head down the drive, and when she went back inside to the kitchen, the screen door bounced shut behind her before she closed the door. The house was silent, except for the ticking of the kitchen clock. But she wouldn't be lonely or bored on her own today. She had dishes to do, breakfast to clean up and a stack of ledgers waiting for her attention on the counter. And next to the ledgers sat that beautifully carved box that her husband had spent a decade finishing for her. She was using it for her recipe cards because she liked looking at it every day. It reminded her of how much her husband loved her, and that reminder was just as sweet today as it was the day she'd come back home.

Miriam stood in the kitchen in absolute silence, her heart soring upward with a silent prayer of thanks. *Gott* had given Miriam the deepest desires of her heart that she'd been too afraid to even ask for. She had her husband, who she loved deeply; she had four sons to call her own, two businesses to grow with the man she loved and a beautiful array of days spreading out in front of her to fill…

She was finally home.

* * * * *

If you enjoyed this story, be sure to pick up these previous books in Patricia Johns's Redemption's Amish Legacies series:

The Nanny's Amish Family
A Precious Christmas Gift

Available now from Love Inspired.

Dear Reader:

We don't all fit into an easy spot, do we? As a romance author, I find it hard to describe myself to new acquaintances. People don't know how to react to "I write books." When I wrote this story, I identified with Miriam a lot. She's strong, smart and just different enough that no one quite understands her.

I truly believe that there aren't any "mistakes" born on this planet. We were given our talents and our personalities for a purpose, and I also believe that God provides us companions for the journey.

So, hang in there, even if you're a little different, like I am. If you'd like to connect, come find me on Facebook, or on my website at patriciajohnsromance.com. I'd love to hear from you!

Patricia

WE HOPE YOU ENJOYED
THIS BOOK FROM

LOVE INSPIRED
INSPIRATIONAL ROMANCE

Uplifting stories of faith, forgiveness and hope.

Fall in love with stories where faith helps guide you through life's challenges, and discover the promise of a new beginning.

6 NEW BOOKS AVAILABLE EVERY MONTH!

COMING NEXT MONTH FROM
Love Inspired

AN AMISH MOTHER FOR HIS TWINS
North Country Amish • by Patricia Davids
Amish widow Maisie Schrock is determined to help raise her late sister's newborn twins, but first she must convince her brother-in-law that she's the best person for the job. Nathan Weaver was devastated when his wife deserted him, but can he trust her identical sister with his children...and his heart?

THEIR SURPRISE AMISH MARRIAGE
by Jocelyn McClay
The last thing Rachel Mast expected was to end up pregnant and married— to her longtime beau's brother. But with her ex abruptly gone from the Amish community, can Rachel and Benjamin Raber build their marriage of convenience into a forever love?

THE MARINE'S MISSION
Rocky Mountain Family • by Deb Kastner
While ex-marine Aaron Jamison always follows orders, an assignment to receive a service dog and evaluate the company isn't his favorite mission— especially when trainer Ruby Winslow insists on giving him a poodle. But training with Ruby and the pup might be just what he needs to get his life back on track...

HER HIDDEN LEGACY
Double R Legacy • by Danica Favorite
To save her magazine, RaeLynn McCoy must write a story about Double R Ranch—and face the estranged family she's never met. But when ranch foreman Hunter Hawkins asks for help caring for the nieces and nephew temporarily in his custody, her plan to do her job and leave without forming attachments becomes impossible...

THE FATHER HE DESERVES
by Lisa Jordan
Returning home, Evan Holland's ready to make amends and heal. But when he discovers Natalie Bishop—the person he hurt most by leaving—has kept a secret all these years, he's not the only one who needs forgiveness. Can he and Natalie reunite to form a family for the son he never knew existed?

A DREAM OF FAMILY
by Jill Weatherholt
All Molly Morgan ever wanted was a family, but after getting left at the altar, she never thought it would happen—until she's selected to adopt little Grace. With her business failing, her dream could still fall through...unless businessman Derek McKinney can help turn her bookstore around in time to give Grace a home.

LOOK FOR THESE AND OTHER LOVE INSPIRED BOOKS WHEREVER BOOKS ARE SOLD, INCLUDING MOST BOOKSTORES, SUPERMARKETS, DISCOUNT STORES AND DRUGSTORES.

LICNM0621

Get 4 FREE REWARDS!

We'll send you 2 FREE Books plus 2 FREE Mystery Gifts.

Love Inspired books feature uplifting stories where faith helps guide you through life's challenges and discover the promise of a new beginning.

FREE
Value Over
$20